Dearest Clementine: Dark and Romantic Monstrous Tales

Candace Robinson

Copyright ©2020 by Candace Robinson
Edited by Luna Imprints
Cover Design by Cover A Day

This is a work of fiction. Names, characters, places and incidents either are the product of the author's imagination or are used fictitiously, and any resemblance to any actual persons, living or dead, events, or locales is entirely coincidental. This book may not be used or reproduced in any manner without written permission from the author.

For those who believe that monsters can love too

♥

Dearest Clementine,

Remember when we first met? You told me you wished I were dead. You thought I had done something I shouldn't have. It was Bogdi, that demon, who harmed your family—not me. I promised myself that he would never bring harm to you again, but somehow it has happened, and he's stolen you away. I want you to know more than anything that you had my heart from the start. Did you see that? I made that rhyme, just for you. If you were here now, you would tell me what a fool I am. I miss that smile, one I haven't seen in weeks. But I'll find you. With everything in me, I'll put an end to Bogdi and help bring you home. Do you want to know a secret? I was going to ask you to marry me, and I'd already written you a collection of stories. You said you did always like my stories, as unconventional as they may be. While we wait, here is the first one, my dearest.

Always Yours,
Dorin

Sail into the Unknown
1872

Keo hadn't known if he was really a boy or a girl when he'd awoken in a small cottage along the side of a dirt road. A woman named Gwendolyn, his mother, had asked him which he preferred to be. When he thought about her question, Keo felt that he was a boy, but he wasn't alive like one. Actually, he was very much alive, only not a human like Gwendolyn.

That day he remembered oh so clearly. The fat moon had hung high in the sky, centered between clusters of shining stars. Even a meteor shower flickered in the distance. It was the day Gwendolyn had brought him to life. The day she became his mother. Kind and smiling, no sign of her vengeful temper. Before the control she had on him. Before the ax.

Gwendolyn had made Keo from an old wooden supper table nineteen years ago, but he never once had come to life. Not until that night. A dark fairy covered in flecks of sparkles that seemed to dance across her skin had entered Gwendolyn's home. Gwendolyn had yearned for a child of her own so badly, and for someone who would help her in her dark tasks. The fairy had chosen to awaken him.

Now, Keo sat propped against the wall, his long gangly arms resting lopsided. Peony, his mother's helper, tapped her foot repeatedly against the spinning wheel as she worked.

His head stayed cocked to the side as he observed her intricate hand movements, his lips aching to move and speak to her. Peony had been working for his mother for the past three months. She was a year younger than him with short, bright-red hair that curled in too many directions, skin dusted with freckles, overly large green eyes, a pointy nose, and plump lips. She was ugly, she was beautiful—Keo couldn't decide—but whatever she was, he felt drawn to her. The wooden heart that beat softly in his chest wanted to call it love, but how could it be so if he'd never truly spoken to her? Yet, he knew that was what it was.

Every other day before she came, he perched himself against the wall to watch her work. Keo could have gone anywhere else—as long as he remained immobile and silent—but he'd chosen to linger in the front room, despite his mother's protests.

The tsking sound continued to echo throughout the cottage as Peony fed the natural fibers into the spinning wheel. Keo's left leg began to cramp until it hurt so much, he shifted to the side to adjust himself. His boot squeaked softly as it rubbed against the wooden floor, but Keo kept his face expressionless.

Peony glanced up from the spinning wheel, her green eyes connecting with his. She gave him a side smile and then continued with her task. Keo didn't know what to think about that strange smile, but he stayed quiet. He could've sworn he heard the ticking of his hard heart clicking against the wood of his chest, but he was only imagining that.

Without peering up again, Peony spoke, "You

know, you can just say something if you want to."

Keo's insides startled, but he remained perfectly still. Was she talking to him? He wanted to look around the room to verify that he was the one she'd spoken to, but he already knew they were the only two inside the cottage. Gwendolyn had gone out to gather fruits and vegetables.

After Peony finished creating the yarn, she stood and brushed the dust from her dark slacks and the edge of her tan tunic. She shuffled toward Keo and knelt directly in front of him, her face only a few inches away. He could hardly breathe.

"I know more than you think I do," she started with that strange smile again, "so you might as well let me see if your tongue is as wooden as your skin."

Keo couldn't contain himself any longer. "You—"

"I knew that would do the trick!" Peony laughed and scooted back.

"How did you—"

"How did I know?" she interrupted again. "A possible secret that I'll save to reveal for another day. All the months I've been here, I've been waiting for you to say *something*."

"You have? But—"

The front door swung open and Peony didn't even flinch. However, Keo did and his mother caught the movement.

Peony gently stood after Gwendolyn walked in. "You're back."

"What are you doing, Peony?" Gwendolyn clenched her jaw, but the words came out sweet. So sweet that Keo could almost taste the sugar cubes soaking in sour milk.

"Oh"—Peony moved toward the spinning wheel, pointing at the fibers—"I just finished up the spool of yarn and was about to head home after I do the last one."

"Haven't I told you not to go near my things?" Gwendolyn's gaze focused on Keo's, as if he was the root cause of all this. Which, he had been.

"He fell and all I did was tilt him back up," Peony explained, crossing her arms. The lie had Keo impressed with the ease of it, the way the words fell from her tongue. *He* even believed it.

Gwendolyn narrowed her dark eyes, moving a strand of gray hair away from her face, and biting her tongue. "I'll see you Friday, Peony."

"Yes, ma'am." Peony didn't even look back once at Keo before she left. He tried not to look at her either, but he failed.

Gwendolyn tap, tap, tapped her heeled boot against the hard floor for several quick beats before speaking. "*Well?*"

"Nothing happened," Keo whispered, trying to make himself believe the words. "I had a cramp and fell to the side, then Peony rushed over and put me back in place. She was probably frightened that if she left me there, you would think she touched your things." Because of the lie, a small fissure cracked on his arm. He wanted to cry, but he held it back.

"She *did* touch my things!" Gwendolyn barked, fists clenched at her sides.

"I suppose you could consider it that way, but nothing happened. She still thinks I'm only a marionette."

Another crack echoed through the house, only this time it was loud enough for Gwendolyn to hear it. Keo wanted to wrap his hand around his thigh, where the wound beat in pain.

"You"—she clicked her tongue and inched toward him—"are a big liar."

Keo kept his mouth shut because if he lied anymore, more cracks would come. It would only make matters worse.

"She dies tonight," Gwendolyn said, her voice tinged with finality.

"But—"

"I was going to have you get rid of Mrs. Krause this evening, but instead, this has to be done. All because you couldn't keep yourself hidden."

Keo gathered all the strength he could to fight back. He stood from the floor, pressing a hand to his leg where the crack lay buried beneath his shorts. "You always say you created me because you loved me," he bit back, "but you created me to be your executioner. Nothing more."

A loud smack radiated throughout the room, and it took Keo a moment to realize it had been his head being pushed to the side by his mother's hand.

Gwendolyn's palm turned beet red, but she didn't seem to notice or care as he pressed his wooden fingertips to his cheek. It wasn't the first time she had hit him, and it wouldn't be the last.

"Tonight will be Peony, and then next week, Mrs. Krause," Gwendolyn said. "After that, it will be whomever I say, for as long as I see fit. Do you understand me?"

Keo blinked his wooden lids. "Yes, Mother." He found it better to agree with her because she would only make him do her tasks anyway, with or without his choosing to. But if he agreed, maybe she wouldn't control him this one time, so he could find a way to escape it.

"You're such a good boy." Gwendolyn pressed the palm of her hand to the cheek she had slapped, before turning to walk into the other room to prepare supper.

"Not always," Keo mumbled to himself, and the crack in his arm closed at the truth of it. "I don't want to live in this house anymore." The wound in his leg returned to perfect condition, the painful throb no longer there.

Somehow Gwendolyn could command him to do anything she wanted. Freewill was something he wished he had, more than being human. He wondered what the taste of that would be. Most likely chocolate and licorice dipped in frosting.

"Oh, and Keo?" His mother came out of the room, wearing her ruffled apron. "Finish making the last spool of yarn that Peony didn't."

His body moved of its own accord. It was a command from his mother and he hated it. Grabbing the fibers from the desk, he sat on the round stool and fed them into the spinning wheel as his booted foot tapped the pedal. Keo worked and worked but grew tired, so he went to the desk where he placed his head against a stack of papers.

"Keo!" Gwendolyn shouted from the other room where she was preparing supper.

With a yawn, he finally lifted his head from the desk, finding his mother already hovering over him. "Yes?"

"You didn't finish." Her tone was condescending and laced with rage.

He looked over at the unfinished spool of yarn. "I'm sorry." A crack tore at his shoulder, creating a sound akin to miniature thunder. He cringed at the bite of pain.

His mother's eyes narrowed, knowing his lie. The one thing he wished he could do, but he couldn't.

"I mean, I was just so tired that I needed to rest my head."

"Grab the ax and go." She smiled with deviousness. "It's time."

Keo's heart and chest tensed up. He wanted so badly to deny what she was forcing him to do. As much as his insides screamed, his eyes glazed over anyway. She was supposed to trust him this time, trust that he would do as she told him to. Even if he wouldn't have. Now there was no choice.

"Yes, Mother." Keo's lips moved, even though it was not him truly speaking. His feet shuffled forward of their own accord and he screamed inside his head, shouting to stop, but he couldn't. His torturous body wouldn't obey his thoughts.

Gwendolyn handed him the ax and he gripped it firmly between his wooden hands. In that moment, he wanted more than anything to take the ax to his mother's arms and legs. She'd made him do things, unspeakable things to the villagers with this ax. It was always removing the head, then the arms, followed by the legs. The images stayed with him, no matter how hard he attempted to block them away. Yet no one in town would ever suspect poor widowed Gwendolyn, or her wooden marionette, would have done something so heinous.

Keo's mother draped his body in a long cloak and placed the fur-lined hood over his head.

"Do me proud, my boy." She patted his back and pushed him through the door. "You will find Peony's house up the dirt road where Mr. Schultz once lived."

Keo knew that house because his mother had made him eliminate the man who refused to purchase yarn from her. But Keo had already known where Peony was staying. He cursed internally over and over as his legs strolled across the field. Nothing he would do could make his body stop. He couldn't feel the grass touching his legs, the wind rumpling his hair, the smell of the outdoors. As his arms moved to prop the ax over his shoulder, all he could do was sit back and watch how everything would unfold.

Everyone in town knew there was a murderer about, but they couldn't figure out who it was. Gwendolyn had told him there were talks of a large burly man with a taste for blood. None of that was true, not even close.

The past year since he'd awoken, he'd been treated this way. Murder after murder, and his control didn't exist in those moments. Even if he'd tried to escape, Gwendolyn could always call him back with the enchantment she had over him.

Up ahead, a small rectangular lantern hung beside a door, where the candle inside burned like a beacon.

The cottage was small and old, but had a coat of fresh paint that he'd seen in daylight. He'd passed by it several times but never ventured close, especially not this close. But oh, how he wished he had, yet not like this. Not with an ax gripped in his wooden-knuckled hands.

He shouted again, trying his hardest to turn himself around. His body didn't listen. It was possible Peony wouldn't be home. It was possible she was with someone having a tumble somewhere else. Anything was possible. If he'd been able to speak the lie aloud, he expected that a crack might have formed right across his chest, exposing his wooden heart.

The sound of his boots hitting the cottage steps boomed in his ears. His torturous hand reached for the door—it must have been locked because he lifted the ax and swung it down to the wood with perfect precision. Keo wondered how he hadn't been caught yet, because sometimes his body did things that weren't the least bit quiet. His commanded self wouldn't have cared, though. It would have swung at anyone who chose to interrupt.

He chopped and chopped—he hoped the sounds would wake Peony if she were home, and give her enough time to escape.

Behind him, feet swished, passing through the grass. His body must have heard it too because it spun around, his hands holding the ax high.

If Keo could truly feel his body, it would have stopped moving. It wasn't a new intruder—Peony stood before him wearing dark trousers and a white tunic, with her short curls messy and sticking up in odd places.

She must have gone out the back and come around to the front, he thought.

The ax went back a few inches more, and he wanted to command his eyes to shut, to not see Peony's beautiful body parts wind up in pieces. Yet, his eyes remained open. He'd have to remember this forever—like the others.

"Keo, stop!" she shouted, holding up a hand, not the least bit afraid.

He waited and waited and waited for the ax to swing down and remove her head, or maybe her arms first this time, or maybe Gwendolyn would choose for him to do the legs instead. But nothing happened. His body stayed frozen like he had wished.

Maybe he could command himself? He tried to wiggle his fingers and not a single one of them even twitched.

With a calm expression, Peony stepped forward and placed her two hands onto his cheeks. He still couldn't move, but he could *feel* the warmth of her hands.

"Keo, come back," she whispered, her green-eyed gaze catching his.

The ax fell from his hands and he took in a deep inhale, and then another, and another. "How ... how do you know my name?" Gwendolyn had never once mentioned the name of her marionette to Peony, and he hadn't stated it earlier when they had spoken for those brief moments.

"You told me earlier, remember?" She smiled and looked away. A lie.

"That isn't the truth," he said, but not moving away from her. "How were you able to command me to stop?"

Peony held up her hand and showed him a bundle of strands of dark hair resting in her palm. His hair. "I've been gathering them, but Gwendolyn's enchantment on her bundle of your hair is incredibly strong."

"Are you trying to command me to do something, too?" he asked in a wary tone.

Shaking her head, Peony leaned forward. "You were able to finally show yourself to me this afternoon—I've had to wait for that. Now I have a proposition for you. How would you like to go to a place where everything from your imagination has a chance of becoming a reality?"

Keo didn't understand why this girl, Peony, wasn't running for the hills or asking him more questions about how a wooden boy was alive. Then thoughts passed through his head, ones of having his own choices to do and be who he wanted to be. A place away from his mother. *His mother...* He remembered something.

"I can't. I'm enchanted here." His voice came out gentle and tinged with sadness.

"Not anymore," Peony started. "With the enchantment I have on this one, as long as we keep our distance, you have nothing to worry about. What do you say?" Her expression looked almost wishful, but how could that be?

Hope stirred in his chest, poking out its timid head. Just as quickly, it was crushed by another thought:

what if Peony was just like Gwendolyn? But if he went back home, it would be an endless life of being his mother's personal executioner. He had to try, try something that would take him away.

And what if this way is worse, Keo? he questioned himself.

Then at least we can say we tried.

He locked his eyes with Peony's green ones once more, struck anew by the familiarity he always felt when looking at her. Before he could haul the words back into his wooden throat, they slipped out. "Lead me anywhere, Flower." Why had he said that?

Instead of frowning at him as he expected, she bowed her head and grinned. "That was just the answer I was searching for." Not leaving Keo a chance to reply to her odd response, she spoke again, "Are you afraid of water? Since your wood might get wet."

"No." He shook his head. "I don't know what I'm afraid of." A sharp pain struck his stomach where a new small fissure had formed. He knew exactly what taunted him when he was asleep and when he was awake. *Gwendolyn*.

Pressing his hand to his abdomen, he followed Peony down the lengthy dirt path that led to the sea. The short journey didn't take long, because the sky still burned with stars and darkness when they arrived. He kept thinking that his body would turn around and go back home, but it never did. His mother must have been too far or Peony's enchantment really was strong.

The sand made soft crunching noises as he stayed close to Peony. She pointed straight ahead and he squinted his eyes to try and see in the dark. As he crept closer, he could see a hidden outline of a raft with a large rectangular sail and human-made tree logs.

"I don't think we will get far in this," he said, stepping to the raft and running his hand against the rickety bottom.

"Keo, how do you think I made it here? It will sail for as long as I command it to." If it were possible, he might have believed that boats had hair to command too, just as she could command him by his strands. He wanted to ask, but he kept his snide comments to himself.

Gripping the back of the raft, he helped Peony push it toward the sea. He hopped on right as it met the small crash of waves. Peony continued to shove it more before finally climbing onto the raft, the bottom portion of her clothing soaking wet. She didn't complain, only stared up at the night sky.

After taking a seat, she reached around and dug through a pack hidden inside a small barrel connected to the pole of the sail.

"Why are you doing this?" Keo finally asked when neither of them laid down to rest. "You know nothing about me, yet you aren't even frightened that I'm alive."

"Why don't you ask me this same question when we make it to the next shore." She shrugged as if that answered everything, when in fact, it only made his head fill with even more questions. Instead of saying anything else, Peony focused on lighting a lantern that she had taken out of her bag earlier.

They sailed farther out into the dark, the lantern staying lit between the two of them. Closing his eyes,

Keo leaned to the side and tried not to think of what he was leaving behind—which was nothing—but that was all that made up his dreams when he drifted off.

One memory, in particular, rose among all others, playing in his dream, turning it into a nightmare.

Giovanni had short-changed Gwendolyn money and refused to pay her the rest, said her yarn was already fraying. Keo's mother grew furious, demanding retribution from Keo. That evening, she sent her marionette—executioner—to take care of Giovanni.

Inside the spacious cottage, it reeked of too-much wine from the bottles Giovanni had spent all his money on. As soon as Keo's ax struck the wood, he knew Giovanni had awoken. He clumsily came to the door with a shotgun in his hand.

Giovanni was too drunk, and Keo was too fast. He slammed the ax against Giovanni's neck and it easily sliced through. Blood flowed toward the surface as the body plummeted to the floor with a loud thump. Arms and legs came next. Slice. Slice. Slice. And slice. Each piece lay a few inches from the body where they were once connected.

Unwillingly, Keo placed the head the same way as if leaving it in a decoration for all to find. All the people he had killed, his enchanted body would leave them this way.

The yells coming from Keo never once stopped.

After standing back up from positioning the body parts, Keo came back to himself. His arms, chest, and face were splashed with scarlet, his hands shaking as he held the ax. He took off on a hard sprint, the opposite direction from his mother's. But the enchantment she had placed on him called him back, causing his feet to lock onto the dirt path. Then, inch by inch, step by step, he was forced to turn around and head home—waiting to perform his next task.

Keo's eyes cracked open to morning and a headful of short red curls. He sat up and stared out at the sea, away from Peony's alluring face. The water was no longer blue, but a dark sparkling purple. He squinted his eyes to get a better look. It wasn't the sea—it was sand. A booming splash sounded from behind him and he twisted his neck in the sea's direction. Out in the distance, protruding from the middle of the sea, was a massive aquamarine beast poking its head above the water.

"That's Charlie." Peony leaped from the raft down to the lavender sand. "He protects our home now."

Around him, the shore itself seemed to breathe and beat its heart as he jumped to the ground beside her. Peony startled Keo by grabbing his hand and yanking him toward rows of tall, thick trees with fat branches and leaves as long as his entire body. To his left were various shades of flowers, some square, others oval, broad, thin, all kinds of assortments. His eyes widened as far as they could go when a pale-yellow flower withdrew itself from the ground, like a sword coming out of its sheath. It diligently walked toward him and bowed.

"Welcome back." The petals moved to form the words.

"What?" Keo's hands shook and he tried to remain calm. While the uniqueness of the situation frightened him, he also recalled it was probably what most humans would feel if they met him—a boy made from wood. Still, the talking plant would take some getting used to. But at that moment, it frightened him all the same.

With a resigned sigh, Peony reached for his wrist. "I was hoping you would remember, but I don't think you ever will." She placed her hands on his cheeks and made him look at her. "Gwendolyn took your memories, and she took you away from us—from me."

Despite Keo's tongue being made from wood, it felt drier than normal, and he feared that this was all a dream. Perhaps he wanted it to be, or perhaps he didn't.

"I wish I could show you my memories but I can't even do that..." Peony took a step back and closed her eyes. Bright blue wings sprouted from her back, ripping the cloth of her shirt. Her short red curls framing her oval face turned to a glossy black, and her eyes changed into the blue of the brightest sky. Even her skin tone gave off a slight pale shade of blue. Peony's face appeared different yet not, still ugly, still beautiful, still imperfectly perfect. A face that could be anything he wished.

"How?" Keo asked, throat dry.

"Gwendolyn, my real mother, not yours, was the ruler here. She created all of us, but this place had had enough of her tyranny and made me its queen. I didn't want it, but you, you were my friend—more than that … you would call me your flower. You worked for her but chose me instead. My real name is Lily, but I changed it to Peony when I disguised myself."

Keo's thoughts shuffled back and forth. He couldn't remember that, none of it. Peony gently placed her hands against his while she smiled, and he pulled away. "The only thing I remember is being a murderer."

Her smile slipped away. "But that isn't you, Keo. You're sweet, and you're kind, and sometimes you do have a bad habit of lying, but only because you don't want to hurt someone's feelings."

Laughter bubbled up his throat and came out in maddened waves. "*Sweet? Nice?* I'm nothing of the kind."

"Do you want to go back to Gwendolyn?" she asked, folding her arms across her chest.

He stared up at the thick trees, then down at the flowers watching him. His eyes were drawn again to the girl he had grown to possibly love just by observing her in his home, the girl who wasn't a girl at all but a blue fairy.

"I don't want to go back home…" This wasn't his home either, not if he couldn't remember anything or anyone. He needed time to think, he needed—Keo's body froze and his arms and legs refused to move.

"Keo?" Peony asked, her eyebrows furrowing. "*Keo?*" she shouted and shook his shoulders.

Unable to answer, he turned around and took off in a jog back to the sea. Keo screamed vehemently inside his head to stop, but he couldn't control it. With his whole being, he wanted to lash out because he knew Gwendolyn had already caught up and found them. He didn't know if Peony had tried to stop him by using her enchanted cluster of his hair, but even if she had, it wasn't working.

Once he exited out from the trees' gargantuan leaves, he could see out into the middle of the sea. Gwendolyn stood on a raft similar to the one that he and Peony had sailed on. Her gray hair blew in the wind as she shifted closer, drawing him nearer, until he met where the sea began.

"Time to go home, Keo!" Gwendolyn shouted.

"He can choose where he wants to go," Peony snapped back, grabbing his wrist.

Keo could do nothing, his body wouldn't go anywhere. It patiently waited for Gwendolyn—who was not his real mother—to come and get him.

"I should have known it was you, Lily," Gwendolyn spat. "You took my land, you took my worker, you took everything!"

"I didn't! The land chose me because you mistreated it—Keo chose me because I loved him!" He could hear the desperation and the sadness in Peony's voice. She loved him?

Keo's legs moved into the water toward Gwendolyn. "Don't listen to her!" Peony called to him, and then toward Gwendolyn she shouted, "Stop, you're going to kill him!"

"That's the only choice now, isn't it?" Gwendolyn seethed. "I always knew he'd be perfect firewood."

There was nothing Keo could do to stop anything, and he felt helpless and useless.

Pulling the strength from somewhere, Peony yanked Keo back and knocked him down onto the sand. She let out a loud whistle that penetrated everything with its intensity, as if it had come from not only her but whatever other inhabitants lived on this land.

Keo's body stood from the ground just in time to see the guardian from the ocean—the one Peony called Charlie—pushing itself upward, jaws unclamping. Trapped inside himself, Keo stared in horrified wonder as the large, deadly beast opened its wide mouth around Gwendolyn's body. Gwendolyn let out a terrified scream as Charlie's sharp teeth met her form with a deafening snap, turning the water red as it sank back into the sea, leaving nothing but blood in its wake.

It took a couple moments but then Keo could move his fingertips, his toes, his eyelids, everything. He turned to Peony and stared in awe.

Her large wings flapped behind her back as her hands flew to her mouth. "Do you remember?"

Keo shut the world out, closed his eyes, and thought for himself until he had his answer. He opened his eyelids and shook his head, knowing it would upset her, but he couldn't lie about this. "No."

Her shoulders slumped, wings sagged, and she nodded. "As I said, I can't return your memories, but I now can give you your body back. If you want it?"

"My body? I'm not made of wood?"

She smiled. "No, you never were. You've been gone a year, and I'm sure Gwendolyn fed you lies about other things that we will have to discuss."

He nodded, willing to rid himself of the shell that

was truly Gwendolyn's executioner.

Peony lifted a hand, causing emerald wings to burst from his back, and the feeling was electrifying. His wooden skin softened and chipped into pieces that collapsed to the sand as his shoulders and body broadened.

He was *real*.

Keo stared at Peony, wishing he could remember his past, but the love had somehow remained. He took her hand into his and kissed it softly. "How about reintroducing me to everyone, Flower?"

Because he couldn't remember her, he knew Peony—Lily—was hurting inside, but she chuckled anyway before taking off on a sprint. "Well, come on, then!"

Even though the past year with Gwendolyn would linger, he'd remind himself every day that he could love himself regardless, until the ugly memories faded as much as they could.

Keo let out a long freeing breath and ran after the girl—fairy—who could one day be his future.

Dearest Clementine,

It's been a few days since I last wrote to you in my journal, and I think I may have a lead. I found your bracelet—the one I made for you—on the porch steps of our cabin in the woods. I'm wearing the one you made for me too, with blue sapphires and golden beads. You always believed because we were fiends, that we weren't good beings, but my dearest, your heart is one of the purest I know. We are demons of a different sort, not like him. Bogdi is the one who is destructive, and if he thinks he can drag you away to the Underworld, then he has another thing coming. This one time, I ask that you darken your heart a bit so you can protect yourself. Until then, my love, I've attached another story. Perhaps you won't be able to hear it now, but one day you will read it.

Always Yours,
Dorin

A Piece for Him
1982

"You can't die!" Talia shouted, shaking the arm of the body in front of her. "You can't!" Releasing Shea's bicep, she slammed her hands against her legs, but he was gone. *Gone.* Something had killed Shea in his sleep. Old age? A heart attack? Talia didn't know, but she had known that one day it would come. Her entire heart felt as if it was broken into two.

She swiped her long black hair from her face and picked up the phone receiver from the cradle to dial an ambulance. With a choked sob, she hung up the phone after calling and clenched Shea's hand once more, holding on tight until the sirens wailed.

Hesitantly letting go of Shea's hand, Talia hurried and flung open the door to let the paramedics inside.

She led them to her and Shea's room. "I-I'm not sure what happened. I went to make him breakfast, and when I came to check on him he was already gone." Despite the need to curl into a ball on the floor and weep, she held her grief in as much as she could.

"Is this your grandpa, Miss?" one of the EMTs asked as he pulled out an object from his bag.

Her spine straightened, and her despair only consumed her further. "No, I'm only his maid." It was a lie. Everything that spilled from her mouth to them was a lie.

Shea had been her lover for years, until he was unable to do much of anything. But she stayed because she loved him, because he was the light she longed to hold onto, and because he was her soulmate if they truly existed.

After all this time, she had found the one.

For the lovers of her past, she had loved them all in her own way. As with Shea, they'd grown wrinkled with graying hair, while she hadn't aged a day. The names repeated over and over in her head. Jasmine, Johnny, William, Laurel, Elizabeth, and on and on and on. Shea…

After the paramedics took Shea's body away, Talia rushed to the only friend she had left. Ednah. Hardly able to see the road through her tears, she sped past a row of old houses and parked in the cracked driveway. Talia scrambled out of the car and jogged to Edna's porch, banging on the door until her friend opened it. Ednah was still in her striped pajamas, and her short gray hair was perfectly set by mounds of hairspray to keep her curls in check.

"What's wrong?" Ednah asked, a wrinkled hand gripping the shirt at her stomach.

"Shea's—" Talia took a deep breath to control herself. "Shea's dead."

Ednah let out a heavy sigh and nodded, because they had both seen it coming. Talia had wanted to believe it would never happen, that it couldn't happen, but Ednah always knew it would.

Talia had met Ednah through Shea who had always been like a sister to him. When Talia told Ednah what she was, she didn't believe it at first, but as the years went by, the old woman had finally accepted it.

The hot tears came again and wouldn't stop. Shea had been everything to her, and the thought of moving on again as she had with the others hurt her more than anything.

She curled up on Ednah's couch, and her friend placed a crocheted blanket over her. The memories of Shea came back to her one after another.

Talia sat on the rocks that formed a straight line from the sand to the ocean, going out about thirty feet before it was only water.

She'd been living in solitude for some time, and she was tired, tired of thinking about where she'd be in a thousand more years. Somehow, she'd been born immortal, whereas her parents had withered and died so incredibly long ago. All of this was beginning to drive her mad. Sucking in a deep breath, she stood from the hard rock and shifted to the very last one. She released her tightened fists at her sides and flexed her hands with her palms outward and stared up at the sky.

"Miss!" a voice yelled. "Miss! Stop!"

Startled, Talia whirled around to see a man running at her wearing trousers and suspenders, with a hat blocking the view of his face.

She cocked her head, but still couldn't see the man clearly. "Yes?"

The man stepped toward her. "If you're looking to drown yourself, that's not the way I would recommend doing it."

Talia let out high-pitched laughter. "Oh, dear sir, are you trying to tell me I can't choose to drown myself if I want to?"

"I wasn't saying that, but I'd have to go in after you, wouldn't I?" He moved to the side, and the sun's rays revealed his face. The man was possibly a little older than her—at least her current appearance—with wide-set brown eyes, tan skin, chiseled cheeks, and a too-long nose.

"Sorry, sir, today is not my day to die. But thank you for your concern." She brushed past him and when she was only a few feet away, he called after her.

"What's your name?"

She spun around and something in his face made her want to possibly see him again. Perhaps it was the crooked smile that made him seem a bit eager. "Save me from the train at the tracks tomorrow, and I might give you a name." Talia smiled in return and walked away.

More memories came to Talia: Shea sweeping her off her feet at the train tracks, him spinning her in circle after circle as they danced to records, her feeding him chocolates, their first kiss at the train station, making love for the first time in the front seat of his car. Then came the bad times: the arguments of why she wouldn't marry him, when she never got pregnant, her confessing to why she could never have his baby because she was immortal, him constantly depressed and afraid she would move on because he was aging.

But the good always overpowered the bad. If only they had both been human, then things would have been perfect.

The day forged into night and Talia fell asleep on the couch. When she opened her eyes, Ednah must have already gone to bed because she was no longer sitting in the worn recliner. Talia stood and turned on the TV, putting it on a channel that was playing *Frankenstein*. It must have been a Frankenstein marathon because a different one played next. After watching the first two, an idea formulated in her head. Something she should have thought about before because Shea loved the films and book so much.

She ran to the bedroom and flicked on the light, finding Ednah on her back with her mouth fully open, lightly snoring.

"Ednah!"

Jerking forward with wide eyes, Ednah's hand flew to her chest. "You can't do that to an old woman," she groaned. "Do you want another person lifeless by the evening?"

Talia was too dead-set on what she came up with to let the words remind her of what had happened to Shea. "I have an idea."

"I'm sure your idea could have waited." Her tone sounded guttural and her eyelids were already starting to close.

"I think… I think I can bring Shea back!" Talia felt this with every fiber in her being that she could. There still had to be enough time.

Ednah sat up wide awake and shook her head. Gently, she pushed her legs to the side of the bed and said in an extremely calm manner, "No, honey, you can't bring him back. Shea is gone."

"I watched *Frankenstein*—"

The old woman held up a hand, interrupting her. "A work of fiction."

"But I know I can help him," she pressed, balling

her fists so tight her palms hurt.

"I'm sorry, child"—Ednah moved from the bed and reached out for Talia—"but we don't have a large electric current machine sitting around, do we?"

Talia drew out of Ednah's warm grasp. "That's not funny, and I'm not a child. I'm hundreds of years older than you."

"Yet you sure don't act it." With a yawn, Ednah sat back down on the bed.

"Fine, stay here," Talia said with anger lacing her words. "I'm going to the cemetery to find a body for Shea."

Not waiting for a reply, she left the room and hurried out to the garage to grab a shovel and an ax before getting into her car. Starting the engine with a loud purr, she headed to the cemetery and held back her tears. It was only a few blocks up the road and no one was ever there, except for the dead.

Under the moonlight's glow, two large metal gates pulled into her periphery. Talia parked the car in the gravelly lot and turned off the headlights. Quickly, she pulled out the flashlight from the glove compartment and collected the shovel and ax from the trunk.

The closer she got, the taller the gate seemed to grow before her eyes. The iron was of a murky black with sharp points and words spread across the top reading, *Morgan's Point Cemetery*. A rusted handle, and no chain, bound it together. She adjusted the shovel and ax at her side and lifted the clasp—a grinding clink filled the air.

She let out a deep breath as if the dead would emerge out of their graves, but they didn't. They remained buried. The only paranormal mystery she'd ever come into contact with was herself.

A slight fog and pine-like scent radiated off the tall trees. She held up the flashlight and scanned the cemetery, stopping on a large rectangular headstone with a crack down the center. An angelic stone angel rested on top, one of its arms missing.

With a hard thrust, Talia stabbed the shovel into the soil. Thankfully, the ground wasn't frozen over so she wouldn't spend days getting to the coffin, but it would be some time by morning. Shovel full after shovel full, she scooped out dirt. The night was already turning into day, and her arms and legs felt like gelatin, but she didn't stop. Not until, finally, the end of her tool struck something solid.

Her earlier sadness had vanished with the new focus driving her entire being, and a new determination was there. Dr. Frankenstein and Dr. Moreau may have been mad, but they were both geniuses who pulled it together. Talia had learned over the centuries that all fiction was rooted in fact. She was living proof of it.

Pulling herself out from the grave, she swiped the ax from the dew-covered grass. She rubbed sweat from her forehead and hopped back into the grave. With one strong whack, she buried the metal end of the ax into the wood. Again, Talia repeated the motion, and again, she hacked at it over and over.

"It took me a few cemeteries to find you, but I'm here," a voice called.

Talia glanced up and tugged the flashlight from her back pocket, pointing the light onto Ednah's face. "What are you doing?"

"I still think you're crazy"—Ednah crossed her arms over her chest as she frowned—"and I still believe that this won't work, but here I am just as Shea would have wanted. He was always such a crazy bastard."

"The craziest," Talia agreed with a smile. As she turned back around, she brought the ax down again and again, thinking about the time she and Shea stood in front of the train until the last second just because they could. Before she could delve further into that memory, the inside of the coffin caught her eye. She threw down the ax and let the rising sun highlight the old bones of a skeleton resting inside.

Ednah perched forward and peered down at Talia and the skeleton. The old woman pointed a painted pink nail at what was the ribcage. "Hmm, are you trying to bring a *skeleton* back to life?"

Tossing the ax and shovel onto the grass, Talia pulled herself from the grave. "No... I don't know! I mean, how long does it take to decompose?"

"By the looks of that skeleton, I'd say it's been decomposed a while." Ednah pushed her glasses up her nose and focused on the tombstone. "Died 1964." Hanging her head and shaking it in disapproval, Ednah continued to stare at the engraving.

Talia gripped her dark hair and dropped to her knees. "I don't know! I'm not a scientist!"

"Well, you sure are trying to be one!" Ednah bit back.

"I can't waste time trying to find skin to wrap around the skeleton, too." Talia had been too desperate to get a body that she hadn't been thinking straight and misread the year on the tombstone. Besides, she didn't know what she thought she would find. Perhaps a perfectly put together body?

"We can fillet my own skin for it." Ednah stared at her, face serious. "I'm sure it will grow back."

"What?" Talia squeaked, her heart accelerating.

"I'm not serious." Ednah scooped up the shovel and turned around. "But I could be…"

"That's not funny!" Talia picked up the ax and followed her friend. The woman was growing closer to death, but she kept her sarcasm strong.

When they made it to the outside of the gate, Ednah closed the metal and pressed down the latch. "Instead of digging for these *fresh* bodies, why aren't you snatching Shea's?"

Talia closed her eyes and bit her lip, turning away from Ednah. "Because… Because I want to give him a new body. One that doesn't hurt."

"What an incredibly beautiful story," Ednah said loudly. "Then how will it be Shea?"

Holding back an inner scream, she twisted around to face her frustrating friend. "I plan on inserting his brain!"

The old woman stabbed the ground with the shovel. "Oh, biscuits and gravy, you really are crazy!"

"It's okay to curse, you know that?" Talia shouted at the top of her lungs. "Fuck! Fuck! *Fuck!*"

Jolting forward, Edna covered Talia's mouth with her wrinkled hand. "Stop! My old ears can't handle it."

"Please help me," Talia mumbled through Ednah's hand.

Closing her eyes, the old woman dropped her hand

and stared at Talia fiercely. "Look, I'm not going to be an accomplice, but I'll drive you to get Shea."

"That's an accomplice."

"No, it's me taking my friend to the funeral home, thinking she's arranging a funeral."

Talia rolled her eyes and headed to her car. First, they dropped off Ednah's Pinto because she didn't want to be seen driving her own, so she drove Talia's.

When they arrived at the funeral home, the building was covered in an off-colored white brick with small windows lining the front.

A single car sat in the parking lot, and Ednah let out a groan, "Well, it was a good try."

Talia looked up and down the sparse street. The funeral home was a lonely building surrounded by even lonelier trees. She knew she could do the job quickly. "I'm going in."

"What do you plan on doing if whoever's in there catches you stealing Shea's brain?" Ednah appeared worried with her lips pursed and wrinkles deepening.

"Murder, if I have to."

"That's a joke, right?"

"What do you think?" Talia smiled and grabbed the dirt-covered shovel from the backseat, along with the ice chest she'd packed. Then she pulled a ski mask over her head and put on a pair of black leather gloves.

At a quick pace, she moved toward the door and knocked rapidly. Several moments passed with no answer. Precious time was slipping away from her. She walked to the grime-covered window and whacked her shovel through it. A ripple of glass rained down between the ground and the inside of the building. She knocked the remaining pieces out, but small chips still nicked her arms and body as she slid inside.

Just as she pulled herself through and lifted the shovel from the floor, the door flung open. Without thinking, she leaped forward and swung the shovel at the interloper's head. A frightened gasp escaped her mouth as the mystery man slumped to the ground.

"Oh fuck. Fuck. Fuck. Maybe I did kill someone on this pursuit." Talia was the real intruder here, but it was her reflexes that did it. She quickly fell to her knees and pressed her hand at the man's throat. A pulse beat beneath her fingers. *Not dead—thank God.* Heart pounding, she rolled him to his side and hastily tied his wrists and feet together with the tape sitting on the desk. The man had gray hair, sunken cheeks, and wore a smock over a long-sleeved collared shirt.

If the man had died, Talia didn't know what she would have done, because her number one concern was getting to Shea's body. She plucked up the ice chest from the ground outside and moved toward the door.

Peeping her head around the open door, Talia didn't know which way to go. In answer, she took the first hall she saw. Pictures of flowers painted the walls, as if the hallway itself was a cemetery. Eventually, she came to an iron door and opened it. Inside, a row of metal stairs led to what she assumed was the basement.

"This must be it," Talia whispered.

A bright light sprinkled across the room, making her eyes squint. Her body stilled and grew rigid when her gaze connected with the silver table. There lay Shea, only him, and no one else. His eyes, always filled with love, now closed forever. His pale skin, once warm, now cold, was already withering. Or maybe that was her imagination. Without touching him, she knew his body was stiff, his skin and everything buried underneath would have no warmth. He looked cold. *So incredibly cold*, she thought. And that left her feeling even more alone.

Once her plan worked, neither would be alone any longer.

A long, clear tube was connected to his right leg. Lifting her mask, she scampered toward him and ripped the tube out and tossed it to the floor.

Talia's eyes filled with tears as she stared at her lover on the table. She would find him a new body. Heart pounding harder, she hurried and set down her ice chest.

Talia had come prepared with tools but the things in the room would work much better. She reached for the bone saw with a sharp circular disk on the end and pressed the yellow button. The metal wheel made a loud buzzing sound, filling the air of the room. If she stuck her finger to it, her digit would be gone in an instant. It was perfect.

Turning the tool off, she stepped behind Shea and pressed her hand to the side of his freezing face. From behind him, she leaned forward and placed a soft kiss on his forehead. "I know you're still in there, so please hold on," Talia whispered.

When she flicked on the tool again, the loud noise filled the room once more. Talia was not a surgeon, but she'd been around long enough to know how to cut something open. However, the task was messier than expected.

As blood dripped and oozed from the incision, she second-guessed herself for a moment, not knowing if she was making a mistake by not attempting to use his old body instead. But she knew Shea, and he wouldn't want this tired body for eternity.

The sound of metal hitting skull only drove her determination further. Once Talia came full circle, she slid off the top portion of the skull, exposing the extraordinary brain. She couldn't help but stare in awe. She'd never seen such a beautiful sight—such a small and wondrous tool could hold so many things. Dreams, nightmares, thoughts, memories, precious, so many precious words exchanged between the two of them.

With careful precision, she pushed her hands in and disconnected the brain as best she could. Talia slowly pulled it out and cradled the organ, studying each indention. From the outside it still looked utterly healthy and perfect. She didn't know if she had done it right, but she made sure to keep it whole.

Bending her left knee, she set it inside the ice chest, along with the bone saw, and quickly closed the lid. Turning away from the body that had grown to give Shea so much pain, Talia dashed out of the room. She wouldn't look back at her lover's body, because the one part of Shea that was truly him was inside the box she carried. His heart was still in his chest, but his true heart that contained what he felt for Talia was buried in the lovely organ she had with her.

Because a small amount of pity washed over her, Talia went out the way she'd come in to check on the man she'd injured. He was still resting on the floor, breathing heavily. To give her more time, just in case, she left his hands and feet taped. Someone would find him, and it wasn't as if he couldn't find a way to slip free if need be.

Talia crawled through the window, leaned in, and grabbed the cooler and shovel. Behind her sat Ednah in the driver's seat, watching her like a hawk. When Talia strolled up, the old woman leaned over and threw open the passenger side.

Taking a seat after placing the shovel in the back, she held onto the cooler tightly, afraid it might disappear if she stuck it behind her or in the trunk.

"Thanks for not helping," Talia said with a small smile.

"You're lucky I'm here." Ednah put the car in drive and glanced at Talia's gloved hands. "Also, you're filthy."

Talia looked down at the red—so much red. "It's blood."

"And it's filthy…"

"We need to find a fresh plot." Talia stared out the window, watching trees wiggle under the wind's strength. "That funeral home didn't have any spare bodies at the moment."

"And what if we dig someone up and he's not up to *par* physical wise, huh?" Ednah snapped.

"This isn't a blind date!"

"It kind of is."

Talia looked down at the box in her lap and rested her cheek against it. "I'll take anyone as long as Shea's in there and he doesn't have to hurt anymore," she whispered, unsure if Ednah had even heard her. All she wanted was to feel Shea's hand gripping hers like it used to.

Ednah stayed quiet for a long time before she finally pressed a palm against Talia's cheek. "I have a better idea."

"I thought you wanted no part of this."

"I don't, but I have a friend who works at the morgue at the hospital…"

Talia straightened and blinked several times before speaking. "What friend?"

"Oh, just someone who comes and goes."

"Like a *special* friend?"

"Something like that." Ednah grinned. "Anyway, we'll go back to my place, you'll get cleaned up, and then we'll go shopping when night falls."

Talia felt as if all the pieces were coming together. She wrapped her hands around the cooler, pressing her head against the plastic. *This is going to work,* she silently told Shea.

Once back at Ednah's home, Talia wiped the blood from the outside of the cooler and took a shower. The water felt cold against her skin—she closed her eyes and thought about Shea.

"Why do you not want to marry me, love?" Shea placed his forehead against Talia's naked shoulder and kissed the side of her neck.

"I just can't…" Talia rolled away from him.

"Is it someone else?" He quickly sat up and ran an agitated hand through his hair. "You can tell me, you know."

"No, there's only you, so stop asking that!" she ground out. "Isn't here and now good enough?"

"But I love you."

"And I'm sure I love you more, that's why I can't." Talia pressed her hand against his warm cheek. He was in need of a shave, but she liked the way the prickly hairs felt against her palm.

He stayed silent.

Softly, she slid her hand away from his cheek and found Shea's hand, interlacing their fingers.

"When you get older, you'll understand."

"When we get older."

"No, Shea, when you get older."

After night bled its inky color over the day sky, Ednah grabbed her keys. "Ready?" she asked, the anxiousness showing in her twitchy hands.

"Yes." Talia's heart had been beating quicker than usual the rest of the day while she'd waited to leave. She grabbed the handle of the cooler because she didn't want something to happen to Shea. Just in case.

Once they got in the car, Ednah sped the entire drive until she arrived at the nearby hospital. It was small compared to the one farther in town with lamps framing the front of the building and two flags flying from their posts.

Ednah looped around the building and took the way that brought them to an open area where the entrance to the basement would be. Outside, a lanky man, a few years younger than Ednah, stood. Talia's breathing increased as Ednah slowed to a stop. The man walked over and shined a flashlight on their faces.

Ednah cranked down the window, its glassy squeak making too much noise. "We're here from the funeral home to pick up a body."

"A body, huh?" The man scratched the side of his balding head. "You know this is illegal."

"Trust me." Ednah reached out and patted the man's forearm. "I'll explain it all to you later."

"This is the guy?" Talia asked.

"So, you've heard about me?" Talia didn't know how to answer his question because she didn't really know anything about this man, but she nodded.

"Julio, I know you're not going to believe me if I explain this to you, but trust me, I'll tell you everything later, like I said. And it will be the real-life miracles you hear about."

The man, Julio, shifted side to side with nervousness. "It's for the funeral home, you say?"

Ednah ticked her head side to side. "The family will thank you for this, I promise."

Talia didn't know what kind of plan Ednah was concocting on her own, but Julio waved them on.

"I suppose I'll go *shop* now, as you suggested." Talia opened the car door and leaned back in. "Are you coming?"

"Nope. Can't be an accomplice." Ednah kept her gaze focused ahead, pretending she couldn't see a thing.

Rolling her eyes, Talia shook her head. "Will you watch over Shea?"

"With my life," Ednah promised.

Talia gently closed the car door and followed behind Julio. He held the door open for her and led her down a long hallway. Her heart pounded as the room grew colder. The fluorescent lights were bright and perfectly lit above. She didn't know what she'd expected. Possibly flickering lights or a dimmer area like in the movies, but the place wasn't any of those things. Only bare white walls and white tile, guiding Talia to her destination.

Julio stopped in front of a door and unlocked it, letting her inside. Before he closed the door, he looked side to side, and said, "Just hurry."

Talia gave a quick nod and slipped farther inside, the quiet enveloping her. Taking in a deep breath and inhaling disinfectant, Talia peered around the room at rows and rows of silver metal drawers. She padded across the linoleum to the first one she saw and drew it open.

In her imagination, Talia assumed all the bodies would look perfect and restful, as if in a sleeping state. However, she knew better, and they weren't. One was a young girl around seven who looked too bloated and too blue. She closed that drawer with a soft click and held her eyes shut for a moment to keep tears from escaping. Another was possibly a man, but Talia couldn't tell because the face was mangled with skin missing in places.

She had thought she could take anyone, but with each person she pictured being Shea, it just ... wasn't. She couldn't imagine any of these hollow bodies opening their eyes or their blue and cracked lips laughing his perfect laugh.

At the end of the row, hands shaking, Talia drew open the next one. Inside rested a man close to her age or at least how old she appeared. Dark hair, brown skin, a wound in the center of his chest from a bullet. She was growing tired and worried and didn't want to keep opening drawers. His body would serve its purpose.

Walking to the door, she cracked it open and said in a professional manner, "I found the one for the funeral home."

Julio didn't look impressed, but he nodded and handed her a clipboard with papers attached. "Just sign this." She grabbed the form and filled it out with lies, all lies.

As she pressed the pen to the form, she nodded to the open drawer. Julio grabbed a rolling table from the corner. Talia set down the clipboard and helped him load the body onto the metal. Anticipation sang in her veins as she followed Julio out the door to her car.

Ednah stayed inside, but the trunk was already popped open. Together, she and Julio loaded the body inside the trunk.

"Why would you risk this?" she asked, closing the trunk.

"I'm old, and there's just something about that woman in the front seat of that car that I can't say no to. I want to live life while I still can."

"Ednah really is something special." Talia smiled. "Thank you."

Julio gave a nod to Ednah and walked away.

As soon as Talia got adjusted back in the car with the cooler in her lap, Ednah asked, "Did it feel as if it was Shea?"

She stared at the cooler as Ednah drove back to the house. "I don't know... It just felt like a body. I thought there would be a connection when I found the one, but I didn't feel anything."

"Better for there not to be one if it doesn't work," Ednah mumbled.

"It *will* work." Talia imagined the body from the morgue wrapping his muscular arms around her, and she brushed the terrifying thoughts away. She instead pictured Shea's warmth coming from within the body, alive and whole, making herself feel better.

When Ednah pulled into the driveway of her house, she looked at Talia. "Can you open the garage?"

Talia hopped out and quickly clasped the handle of the garage, then pushed it up, allowing the rickety sounds to echo. She thought the old garage would collapse, but it stayed up as Ednah backed the car inside.

Setting the cooler aside and closing the garage, Talia and Ednah hauled the heavy body out of the car as best they could, propping him on the ground. Then Talia grabbed the cooler, placed it beside the man, and gathered the tools from the bag she'd left on the small table.

"I can help you stitch," Ednah said.

With a brief nod, Talia began working. She flipped on the tool she'd taken from the funeral home and let the buzzing block any noise as she concentrated on cutting the skull. Talia pressed her fingers in between the skull and removed the old brain. Ednah already had the cooler open and Talia rested the old one on the lid and picked up Shea's.

Blowing her hair out of her face, she inserted Shea's brain. If everything went well it should align and attach of its own accord.

Ednah had been a nurse during the war and afterward had become a seamstress, so Talia watched as she sewed up the nameless man with precision right by the hairline.

"What are you going to use for the electricity?" Ednah asked. Talia expected her friend's tone to be condescending, but it wasn't. She appeared more curious than anything.

"My heart," Talia murmured as she gazed into the closed eyes of the man she hoped would be Shea.

"*What?*" Ednah screeched and covered her mouth.

"My heart." Talia locked her gaze on Ednah's. "It's immortal, right? I want you to split it into two."

"That…" Ednah shook her head. "That's not going to work. You'll both be dead!"

"Then it might be better that way." Talia shrugged and looked away. She'd already lived such a long life. Some of it good, some of it bad, and some of it wondrous. If it had to end tonight, then that's how it would be. She truly believed in soulmates and Shea was hers. An eternity without her other half wouldn't be one worth living at all. Her heart was useless without his anyway.

Despite the horrified look on Ednah's face, Talia grabbed a scalpel from the bag and made an incision on the chest of the nameless body. After pulling back the skin, it took her a bit to find the organ, but she wrapped her hands around the heart and took it out.

She set the dead organ in the cooler.

"I'll have to figure out how to dispose of those," Ednah said.

But Talia ignored her and removed her shirt, tossing the fabric to the ground.

"You're not really going to do this, are you?" Ednah pressed, stepping closer.

"I am." Her bra came next, and she placed a shaky hand at her chest, clenching the scalpel. "Okay, I may need a little help here."

"Whiskey?"

Talia shook as she nodded. "That would be nice." She didn't move a single inch as Ednah went inside and rushed back out with a glass bottle in one hand and a bottle of pain meds in the other.

Talia grabbed the bottle of liquid and downed the whole thing before pressing the blade to her chest. Its coolness caused her nerves to quake.

"I'm going to have to finish this, I assume?"

"Yes," Talia started, "but you'll only have to cut my heart into two and place a piece in mine. I'll finish the rest, if it works."

"What if I don't cut it perfectly in half?" Ednah gritted her teeth, her brow furrowed, thick beads of sweat coating her wrinkled face. "What if I do too much or too little?"

"Do your best."

Nervously, Talia slid the scalpel down her chest. Warm blood bubbled up but it was as if she didn't feel the pain, or maybe she chose to ignore it because she knew something better and extraordinary might happen. Clenching her jaw, she pushed her hand inside until she cradled her palm around her own heart, feeling the beats pump against her closed fist.

"For Shea." Then she ripped it out and the world fell to a rainbow of colorful pieces.

Talia's eyes flicked open to a creamy white ceiling with black smudges in various places. Her breathing came out in rapid waves and her chest ached. She let her head fall to the side to see Ednah staring down at her.

"Don't make me do anything like that again," the old woman said, attempting to look angry, but Talia heard the worry. "My old heart can't handle it."

Talia peered down at her newly stitched-up chest. Ednah quickly tied off the string and stepped back. Sitting up, Talia placed her hand to her naked chest and her heart beat with a healthy *thump*. It felt the same.

Ednah handed Talia her shirt, and she slid it on. "Where's the other half?"

"I set it inside the cooler."

Licking her dry lips, Talia leaned over the cooler and fished out the other half of her own bloody heart. She gave an inner prayer to whoever her maker was and wished more than anything to hear Shea's voice.

The body lay as it had before, and she moved skin and muscle back, sliding the heart inside Shea's new chest.

"I don't care what you are as long as we're

together." His words played over and over in her head.

And before she let go, a teeny pulse thrummed against her hand. With a wide smile, her head turned to Ednah. "I told you it would work!"

The old woman pursed her lips. "Remember, *Frankenstein*?"

Talia knew she was thinking about Dr. Frankenstein bringing back a monster who wasn't like he should have been, but in the book it was different. "Hollywood always exaggerates things."

"Sometimes." Ednah walked forward and bent low to stitch up the chest. The eyes burst open, the body jolting upward.

A small yelp came from Ednah but Talia yelled, "Don't move!" She didn't want something to go wrong now.

The stranger's dark brown eyes shifted to Talia, focusing on her. His shapely lips parted, the deadness of his skin was already turning a healthy glow. "T— Talia?"

Talia clasped her hands together with hope, fighting back the tears that were coming. "Shea?"

"Yes?"

"Just lie down and let Ednah finish with your chest. It will sting a bit." *Or more than a bit,* she thought.

No one spoke as Ednah worked with hurried motions. Shea appeared confused but didn't take his dark eyes away from her.

"I'll give you two a minute," Ednah said when she tied off the string before heading inside.

Shea still hadn't said anything else, but he had spoken her name earlier. What if he slipped into the monster from the movies as Ednah had said?

Finally, Shea brought a hand to his jaw and rubbed the way he always did when he was nervous. "Talia, what's going on? I don't... I don't feel like me."

Worry washed over her because what if he didn't like the body he was in? "You died, and I brought you back in another body by putting your brain inside."

He stared at her, his eyes ticking side to side, still rubbing his jaw.

"I gave you a piece of my immortal heart, so if all goes as I think it will, you're going to be immortal, too." The next part was hard to say, but she would do anything he wanted, whatever would make him happy. Just as he'd always put her first. "But, if you don't want it, I can take it out." She removed her gaze from his and stared at the cement.

"Hold on a minute, you cut out a piece of your heart ... and put it in here"—he tapped at his chest and then at his skull—"along with my brain?"

"Mmm hmm..." She still couldn't meet his gaze.

"Okay, you're going to have to give me a moment here ... or several." He propped his back against the car. "I feel like I can do things again if I want to. As if I can jump off the roof and not break a leg."

"Oh, you would still break a leg, Shea." Talia smiled. She'd been worried for no reason because even with the new body, it was absolutely Shea. He was here with her. "Are you mad at me?"

He shook his head as tears filled his eyes. "No, of course not. But how could you risk your life like that for me? I—I'm nothing compared to you. You've always been everything to me. Please promise me you won't ever do anything like that again."

"Could you promise me the same?" She already knew what his answer would be.

Shea bit his lip and stared down at his new hands. "Never."

"Then we're even." Talia's half-heart thumped hard against her ribcage—she couldn't believe he was really here. All she wanted to do was touch him, and never stop.

His gaze caught hers and an old and familiar feeling seemed to swell between the two of them. "I suppose all that matters is that I'm here alive and with you. There's nothing better than that."

"Is there anything you want to do in your new body?" she asked, arching a brow. "Go ride a bike?"

"Well, it's been a while since we…" He leaned forward, the left side of his lips tilting up.

"Shea, you dirty rascal." Talia gave a false huff and placed her hands on her hips.

Before Talia could gather her thoughts, Shea scooped her up from the ground. Laughter bubbled up from her, and she wrapped her arms around his warm neck. "Ednah's inside."

"Trust me, she'll understand."

She looked at the crimson by his hairline and the red on her hands and arms. "We have blood all over us."

"Eh, a little dried blood never hurt anyone."

"Seriously, shower first."

"Fine." He pulled her closer and she relaxed in his arms as he murmured in her ear, "I love you."

"You have my heart forever, so I *suppose* I feel the

same…" Talia grinned.

His chest pressed against hers and it was as if she could feel his heart, her old heart, beating for the two of them.

Dearest Clementine,

My beautiful, beautiful love. I was so incredibly close. I found the secluded house where Bogdi was keeping you. I'm here now, but you're already gone. Your cinnamon scent mixed with lilies still lingers—an aroma that could entice me to no end. However, there is also the odor of rot coming from Bogdi, radiating from the floorboards. You and I are equals—a team—and I will stalk the countryside to get you back. I know he's trying to find a way to drag you to the depths of the Underworld, but we have to stop him. I promise with everything in me, that the demon will be sorry. I have a tale for you now, one I know you would love.

Always Yours,
Dorin

Lured in for Death
2012

*M*arch Martinez sat cross-legged while thinking in front of the lake, surrounded by miles and miles of trees. If only this place held the answers to his questions about life. As the water's ripples swished back and forth, he thought about the mysterious vanishings. This particular lake had been searched thoroughly over the years when claims surfaced about people disappearing. Some said that people had gone in but never came out. But the thing was, when police investigated the lake, no victims were ever found.

He stood from the pebbled dirt and peered down into the clear water—no sign of life, not even a single small fish or minnow wiggled about.

March felt alone, so alone it was hard for him to breathe anymore. His breath came out ragged, his heart accelerated, his thoughts progressed with intense fury and wouldn't stop. Each morning he told himself over and over how much he wanted to live, but finding that drive was becoming more difficult day after day, after long day.

Closing his eyes for a moment before reopening them, March tore off his T-shirt and unbuttoned his pants to slide them down, until the only clothing covering him was his boxers.

With a leap of faith and a wish for something that

wasn't suffocating, he jumped into the water, letting his body sink to the bottom. Disappointment filled him when he opened his eyes—there was nothing magical or a chance at escape, only a pebbled bottom surface and the late afternoon sky glowing above.

March prayed for something hidden, something *other* than what was here. And even more, he wished—he *yearned*—for whatever was down there to take him away from all the hurt, the pain, and his thoughts. He continued to hold his breath until he couldn't anymore, until his body surfaced back through the top layer of the lake.

A deep agonizing exhale escaped March's throat as the water swished back and forth, crashing against his shoulders. In that moment, he knew there was nothing. In that moment, he knew he was the only one who could save himself. But could he even do that?

March pulled himself from the water and rolled to his back, staring up at the hovering sun that would be descending soon. His cell phone rang from the porch of the cabin, causing him to jerk forward. He hurried to scoop up his clothing, briskly jogging to the porch steps. As soon as he picked up the phone, the rings ended. Then it started again, and Joseph's name appeared—his brother.

"Hello?" he answered, his voice coming out raspy from his dry throat.

"Marcin?" Joseph said, his tone filled with eagerness and a suppressed sound that resembled something akin to fear.

March didn't want his brother to worry—he was tired of making him and his parents concerned about him. So he put on the best act he could while his insides still felt tender. "Who else would be answering my phone?"

"What's going on, then? You didn't text me back."

"I rented a cabin for the weekend, remember?" March pressed his head to the wooden pole connecting the roof to the porch. "I'll be home soon."

"Oh, yeah, I totally forgot. I was checking to see if you wanted to come over for video games, but maybe next weekend?"

"Of course. Wouldn't miss it for the world. Bye, Joseph." March ended the call, sickened with himself for having to put on a brave face for everyone. He didn't know if he'd be alive next weekend. Hell, he didn't know if he'd be alive tomorrow.

A pulse formed in his temples and he wanted to scream and cry in frustration like a child, as if he wasn't a twenty-four-year-old man. If it wasn't one thing, it was another—his life was becoming more and more affected by the migraines, by his anti-social behavior. March had never had any real relationships. He'd only had sex twice, and even that was with guys he'd met online, strangers who'd lost interest afterward.

Pushing off from the beam, March pressed himself inside the cabin. The coolness of the air hit him and sent a shiver throughout his body. It wasn't cold enough to start a fire, but he wanted to feel the warmth anyway. After spreading out his damp clothes on a wooden bench near the entry, he set several logs in the fireplace and started the kindling.

March placed a few blankets from the couch on the

floor and sat back, pulling his knees to his chest. Twenty-five years old in only a couple of weeks. He stared down at the jagged scars on both his wrists, the memories rippling through him. His family had never been a factor in why he felt the way he did, because they had always been great—perfect, even. It was something wrong with him, something he was trying to fix. Trying so damn hard.

A clink came from across the room. With tears sliding down his cheeks, March glanced over his shoulder. Out the window was an outline of someone looking in—a man—but he couldn't see him clearly.

"Hey!" March shouted, jumping to his feet. He threw open the door and found the porch empty. In the distance, he heard a loud splash from the lake.

Without pause, March took off running, searching for the man who had jumped into the water. As the lake neared, he didn't hesitate, and dove into the clear liquid. Once below the surface, he twisted and turned as the water swirled around him, but only the pebbled rocks of the bottom surrounded him.

Gliding his arms through the water, he surfaced and blew out unfocused breaths, when something light brushed his ankle, as if a finger had stroked him. He dove down under again, exploring every direction he could, discovering nothing.

Frantic, March shakily swam back and pushed himself from the lake to return inside. On the way to the cabin, he looked all around, thinking that his mind was playing tricks with him. His head still pounded, so it was possible.

Once inside, he removed his boxers and took a

couple pain pills for his migraine. He grabbed a blanket from the floor, cocooning himself inside and watched the fire, pretending nothing had happened.

Bang! March's eyes flew open to the loud noise. He scrambled to his feet and gazed up at the roof where the sound had come from. The flames in the fireplace had already died out, and the sun was gone for the day.

March cocked his head and listened for another bang and when nothing came, he lifted his phone from the table and checked the time. It was a little after one in the morning. He was about to lie back down and chalk it up to his imagination when another bang blasted from the roof. His gaze flicked to the ceiling once again and remained locked there. He didn't know if he was scared or annoyed, but his body stayed frozen.

Screeeeeeeech! The shingles to the roof sounded as though they were being clawed. March dropped the blanket and threw on his still-damp clothing from the bench, then flipped on the living room light. With a few quick swipes, he turned the flashlight on from his phone and ran outside, barefoot.

The light on his cell wasn't bright enough, but the sky above was decorated with illuminating stars that he wasn't used to. In his hometown, they were always buried by pollution. Taking several steps backward, he craned his neck to get a clear view of the roof.

"Hello?" March rasped, automatically feeling dumb for asking that. It was probably only a raccoon—there were lots of animals here compared to his apartment back home. If it wasn't an animal then a normal person wouldn't have come outside empty-handed, but he wasn't afraid of dying. Regardless, death would come for him one day. Even when he had wanted death to come, the Reaper had still left him behind.

Tilting his head, March tried to listen for any more rumblings. Only the calming breeze, a hooting owl in the distance, and the singing of insects pulsated in the darkness. He shook his head and went back up the few steps, but a crash to the ground caused him to whirl around.

March brought up the phone flashlight in a hurry, only catching a glimpse of pale skin and jet-black hair as something dashed at an intense speed toward the lake. It was too dark to see anything farther out as the smack of water echoed.

His pulse raced with a feeling March could only identify as longing. For what, he wasn't sure. Maybe he'd wanted whatever had been on that roof to take him somewhere in that lake, too. Maybe his headaches were causing him to not only *feel* things, but to see them. March didn't care. He strode toward the lake, knowing there could be a huge possibility that he would end up dead.

The lake stood in front of him—the reflection of silvery stars and the thin sliver of the crescent moon glittered across its surface. His heart gave a delicious pound of fear of the unknown, the intrigue, the want, the hope, and possibly the appetite.

Despite his earlier trembling, March now had a steady hand when he set his phone on the edge of the lake and toed his way in, water kissing knees, waist, chest, then neck. With gentle movements, he treaded farther out into the lake. *Waiting. Waiting. Waiting.* Closing his eyelids, March let himself sink down, down, down. He opened his eyes, but at night all he could see was darkness shrouding him in a thick cloud of liquid. His heart sped up as he kept his eyes open, staring straight ahead into the murkiness. It felt as if maybe something was in front of him, or maybe he only wished it.

March reached a hand, prepared for something, but only the bend and stretch of water brushed his fingertips. He needed oxygen and couldn't hold his breath any longer. Out of his control, March moved toward the surface. But just as he felt the night air on his head, something cold latched tightly around his foot and pulled him back under, preventing his escape.

As the air left his lungs, he couldn't bring himself to scream. Not even as he was being dragged downward, farther and farther than he believed the lake could ever go. His heart beat wildly, lungs burning, and still he smiled as he waited for death to take him, the world turning blacker than it already was.

March opened his eyes and saw an angel. Large silvery

eyes looked into his, staring down at him with an unreadable emotion. His skin was pale white, like the color of the moon. Long dark hair flowed past his shoulders. But March couldn't stop staring at his face, the broad nose, the sharp canine teeth. Two separate necklaces with arrowheads hung from the stranger's neck against his well-sculpted, naked chest. All he wore was a pair of cotton pants and no shoes.

While still dazed, March thought he'd woken in Heaven with a man who could fulfill every single one of his desires. But then he remembered the lake and everything that came before that. March opened his mouth to shout, but the man's hand slammed around his lips. "Do not shout. If you do, he will come, and trust me, you will not like what he does to you."

With a robotic nod, March took a deep swallow. He had asked for death, wanted death, but instead, he'd woken up somewhere else.

"Where am I?" March mumbled, looking around the small room. Dirt covered the rounded ceiling and uneven walls. It was all empty—no photographs, no memorabilia, nothing.

"You are nowhere," the man answered, fully withdrawing his hand from March's lips.

"I need to leave." If he had to be awake—*alive*—he couldn't stay in this unfamiliar place. He nudged the panic back down that attempted to rise.

The man shook his head and shrugged. "Once you're here, you're always here." It wasn't a threat, more of a resolved matter.

March sat up and got a good look at the man. The pale skin, the dark hair—he recognized him. "You're the one I saw in the window, who leapt from the cabin. Who are you?"

"My name is Ira." He paused, clenching his jaw yet his tone dripped with melancholy from his next words. "And I came back here, did I not?"

A loud scream echoed from outside the room, startling them both. March jolted forward and Ira placed a hand against March's chest.

"What is that?" March whispered.

Ira pressed a finger to his own lips and spoke softly. "One of his victims."

Victims? March stood from the ground and backed up until he hit the dirt wall. To his left, small drops of water leaked from the ceiling in the corner.

"You wanted to die..." Ira said.

"I did." What he wanted was to fade out and never awaken again. This seemed more like Hell. Maybe that's where he was.

"Do you no longer wish this?"

"I-I…" In that moment, March didn't know what he wanted. He knew he wanted to go home, though.

The screaming from outside of the room started again, louder than before, and not stopping. March had to do something. He couldn't just sit here listening to someone scream in unimaginable pain. Holding his breath, he hurried past Ira.

Ira attempted to grab him, his face full of concern. "You can't."

March didn't stop as he ran out into the hall. People stood against a long dirt corridor lit with metal torches, burning warm blue fire. The people's arms remained neatly at their sides, as if in a trance.

Ira came up behind him and spoke softly, "Stay quiet."

March nodded and waved his hand back and forth in front of a man covered in tattoos with a shaved head. The man didn't even blink. March shifted to the next person, a woman with long brown curls and mahogany skin—she didn't respond either. Neither did the next, or the next.

As though it were a sense of duty, he moved down the line toward the screams. Ira remained close behind him every step of the way. He wished he was brave enough to swoop in there and stop whatever was going on, but there were those who were courageous like in the comic books, then there were people like him. Ones who were frightened to be noticed.

Yet he pushed himself farther and farther until he came to an open archway. The screaming intensified. March took a step forward and peered around the opening. Inside, people sat against the walls. Except the walls weren't dirt-colored, they were stained with bright red blood. Fresh blood. A head lay on the floor, ripped clean from a body, its terrified eyes staring at nothing, its hair soaked in blood. The screaming had stopped, but March couldn't get a clear view of the rest of the victim's body. In front of the slain man stood a creature with skin so pale it was translucent, its skeleton visible beneath blue-black wings that nearly dragged the blood-covered floor. Hair like ragged darkness hung past gore-splattered shoulders, while its muscular legs ended at clawed feet. Its head turned to glance over its shoulder—

Two large hands pulled March back and covered

his mouth again. "Don't," warm breath whispered against his ear, tickling it.

Ira slowly led March back to the room, passing the line of zombie-like people.

"What is that?" March asked, more in shock than anything, when they came back into the original room. His body didn't give the slightest tremble, as if it was all a dream.

"An underground demon—some of you people whisper vampire before going into your trance," Ira murmured. "This is a demon who will rip your head straight from your neck and lap all the blood he can savor—one who will hypnotize you when he so chooses and then have his way with you."

"How do you know this?" March asked, trying to block out all the ways the demon would have his way with him if he got his hands on him. His hands automatically went to the back of his head as if that would keep it attached.

"My mother was his sister..." Ira bit his lip, displaying one of his long canines. "She got pregnant with me from a human."

"Where is she?"

"Dead. He consumed her," Ira said flatly, but there was hurt that flickered behind those silver irises.

March's eyes widened. "What's going on with those people out there?" He didn't know anything about Ira, but he hadn't killed March yet.

"It will be you in a few days when he comes searching and locks his eyes with yours..."

"Well, why the fuck did you drag me down here?" March asked, trying to keep his voice as low as possible, even though he felt anger blooming.

"Because you kept going into the lake, asking for death!" Ira whisper-shouted, stepping too close to March. "I let you go numerous times."

March pressed his hands to his forehead and slid them down his face. It was his own damn fault he was in this position. "What about you? Do you like being here? Do you want to leave?"

"It's the only thing I've wanted, but the underground demon has all the control. I venture out through different bodies of water to scavenge for him. I hate it." Ira's silvery gaze met March's, and there was something there, a longing for a different sort of life. "He hasn't seen you yet, so there's a chance I can take you back. If not, then… Well, you saw what happens."

An image of his own head being ripped off and a tongue circling inside the open wound appeared. March pushed it away. "What about you?"

"I'll continue doing what I do." A solemn expression crossed Ira's angelic face as his eyebrows furrowed.

March stared around the empty room. It didn't seem like much of a life for Ira—it seemed more horrible than his. He had always thought at times that his life was far worse than anyone else's, even though he knew it wasn't true. It was just something inside himself that needed to be mended.

"You can come back home with me?" He didn't know why he was asking this person—half underground demon—to come back with him.

"My blood is bound to his," Ira said.

"Can you bind it to someone else instead?"

"I can, but I would still be bound to someone else."

March thought about the choices of being bound to that demon in the other room or to a human. It seemed like a pretty obvious choice to him, but perhaps Ira didn't know better.

"Look, Ira," March started. "I'm not much, but you could bind yourself to me and then we can get the hell out of here. I promise I won't force you to do shit, all right?"

A new scream radiated throughout the underground corridor, a woman this time.

Ira peered down at March. "I don't know—"

"What do we need to do?" With the screams going on, March was getting desperate, and Ira needed to answer faster.

"Drink each other's blood."

"Fucked up enough, but let's do it." March wasn't scared about swapping a little blood—he was more worried about getting his head ripped off.

A hint of amusement spread across Ira's face. He grabbed March's wrist and his gaze softened as it locked onto the scars. "What happened here?"

"Self-inflicted." March's eyes didn't shy away from Ira's. When people asked about his scars, March always told them the truth, whether he felt ashamed or not.

Ira pulled one of the arrowhead necklaces from around his neck. "Do you want it here"—he ran a fingertip gently at the scars on March's wrists and then ever so slowly at March's neck—"or do you want it here?"

"A scar is a scar." Another one to add to his old

collection. But he couldn't help but like the way Ira's fingertip felt against his skin.

Ira's eyes lingered a beat too long on March's neck and swiftly drew a line across March's scars at his left wrist. Closing his eyes, March bit his lip at the stinging sensation.

Compared to the calluses of March's fingertips from his years with the violin, Ira's hands were soft. When Ira's warm lips wrapped around his scarred wrist, he opened his eyes. March felt no pleasure from the suction as he'd seen in movies with vampires. But when Ira lifted his head and ran the tip of his tongue across the wound where blood was dripping, something about that movement made his heart pound a little harder and his pants grow a little tighter. His other hand brushed Ira's chest and he felt him shiver.

Ira handed the arrowhead to March with a small smile.

"Where do you want it?" March asked.

"Neck is fine." Ira cocked his head and faced away from him. However, March could feel Ira's eyes trying to study him.

March's hand didn't shake because he'd cut flesh before. It wasn't as if it was hard and he knew how deep to go. He bent his knees a fraction so he could meet the spot where the blood bloomed. With a deep breath, he leaned forward and sucked in the liquid's warmth, not the least turned on by that either. But parts of him hardened at the softness of Ira's skin and how one of the half demon's hands lingered at March's waist, stroking his thumb back and forth.

It was the wrong time for March to lust for a

stranger, but he felt it nonetheless. He pulled away and backed up a few steps. "Is that it?"

"Yes," Ira said, chest heaving, "but we need to hurry. The blood should also help so you won't fall under his spell."

March squeezed the arrowhead in his hand and noticed that the screaming had stopped. No one was making a single sound out in the corridor. They quietly slipped out of the room and March looked to his right, seeing people still lined up against the wall. Before his head could fully shift to his left, something hard slammed into his shoulder, pushing him up against the wall. He couldn't see who it was, but he knew it was the underground demon. The flap of the demon's wings echoed around the corridor.

From up ahead, Ira whirled around, with his eyebrows raised all the way up, and mouthed, *Don't move*. March didn't think he could move if he tried.

"What is this?" a deep voice slurred at his ear. March could smell the scent of blood wafting off the demon.

"One of your feasts, my lord," Ira said, sauntering closer.

"Why is he following you?" the demon's voice boomed, deep with rage.

Before Ira could speak, the demon flipped March around to face him. March stood as still as he could, trying to appear glazed and unfocused like the others decorating the corridor. He silently prayed the blood worked and he wouldn't become the demon's bloody plaything.

The demon's eyes were large like Ira's, except

their color was a bright, glowing red. His nose curved and came to a long point.

"I want this one next," the demon cooed, inching closer so that their noses almost touched. March had heard of people pissing their pants when frightened. He never thought it was true until that very moment when he thought he might not be able to control himself.

"You have a line waiting." Ira motioned up ahead at the others.

"No," the demon said. "I think this one will be sufficient."

The arrowhead was still clenched in March's hand and with all the courage he had, he shoved it into the side of the demon's neck and took off on the quickest sprint of his life. Ira caught up and grabbed March's hand and pulled him even faster.

Behind them, the pounding and beating of the demon's wings echoed, nearer than March would have liked.

Up ahead a lake sparkled and Ira shouted, "Hold your breath."

They barreled into the lake, Ira wrapping his arms around March's waist. Automatically, March kicked his legs as Ira propelled them forward. The dark water made it so he couldn't see anything, least of all where they were headed.

Eventually, above them, a small amount of light filtered through what might have been a door of sorts. Ira pushed it open, breaking them through. March's lungs started to burn and he needed air, but he held on as much as he could.

The water became no longer dark, but clear—

familiar. The lake. *His* lake.

In his head, March counted as the surface came closer and closer. *Four. Three. Two. One.* His face hit air and he took in a deep inhale, the oxygen like a true feast. Ira flung March onto the shore and right as he stuck his hand out to Ira, the half-demon was sucked back into the depths.

Frantically, March searched around, knowing he could take off running—but he didn't. He clumsily jumped back into the lake and swam until he could see the demon clasped onto Ira's leg, trying to yank him back under. The demon's wings beat against the water, creating thick waves.

March sliced through the liquid, getting as close as he could. With a tight fist, he punched the underground demon in the face. It barely moved. The demon turned his head to look at March as in, *What the fuck did you just do?* March wanted to ask himself the same question.

The demon's clawed hand came around March's throat, crushing like a vise, choking him. Ira rushed between them, ripping the second arrowhead from around his own neck before plunging it into the translucent skin just below the creature's ear. Blood mixed with the water as March found the opportunity to slam his foot into the demon's stomach.

Angry bubbles escaped the demon's hideous mouth as he screamed. March felt the creature's grip loosen from his neck as the demon sank, falling, flailing furiously at his wound. Ira kicked the demon viciously in the head—once, twice—driving the struggling creature deeper into the darkness.

Ira grasped March's hand in his, both kicking their legs without turning back. March wanted to lean into Ira's strength as he carried him forward, pulling him upward, toward the surface.

Hands shaking, March fell to the ground, breathing heavily as he scooted back away from the lake. "Is the demon dead?"

"No." Ira shook his head. "He can't die."

"But you can?" March knew Ira was half human so it was possible.

He shook his head again and lowered it, then placed his hand in March's, squeezing it tightly. "And neither can you. But we have to go before he finds a new helper—underground demons cannot last too long in the air above the surface. That's why he refuses to come out."

March didn't hesitate and ran, not releasing his hold on Ira's hand. All he had ever wanted in the world was to die, but in that moment, March truly wanted to live. He had Ira to thank for that. Their story together wouldn't end here. Bound together forever, it had only just begun.

Dearest Clementine,

I'm going positively mad without you. I feel as if I can hear you screaming in my sleep, and when I'm awake, I can hear you everywhere! My fiend heart is crying for you, too. Wherever you are, I hope you hear my words of encouragement. Who would have thought that fiends could love so deeply? You saved me. Did I ever tell you that? You rescued me from myself when I felt so incredibly alone. It was because of you, and it always will be, my beautiful darling. For now, my dearest, this story is for you. You did always like a good ghost story.

Always Yours,
Dorin

Darkness Can Be Good
1942

From the pot on top of the stove, Frankie ladled the steaming stew into a ceramic bowl. Her hand cramped up, causing a bit to splash on the hardwood floor.

"Drats," she said as she bent down and cleaned the spill with the edge of her apron. She stood back up, a dizzy spell washing over her, and her body swayed from side to side. She'd been getting these episodes for the past week. The same thing had happened to her sisters. First came Anna with her bright smile, then Julia with her caring heart, and then Wendy with her curious questions. Now, it seemed to be happening to her.

Frankie and Wendy were the only two left, though. Anna and Julia had already passed into the next world.

"Are you all right?" The shout came from the sitting room—her Aunt Gemma. She heard the creak of her aunt's rocking chair as the older woman sat in her usual place by the fire, her slippered feet moving her back and forth as her wrinkled hands stitched endless blankets.

"I'm fine, Auntie," Frankie called back, holding the hot stew in between her palms. "Thank you."

After Frankie and her sisters' parents died, Aunt Gemma had taken the four of them into her home. It had been tough adjusting at first but, as time went by, things got better—until the illnesses struck.

"You're moving too slowly," Felisha said, her cousin brushing past her to go into the sitting room, not stopping to lift a finger to help. Her cousin was more like the evil stepsisters in *Cinderella*. Lazy and a-good-for-nothing. Always playing with her bright red hair or putting on makeup in the mirror.

Frankie wanted to yell at Felisha's back, but it would do nothing. There were times when Frankie felt she was too nice, but sometimes, she didn't want to be that way anymore. And Felisha didn't help in that matter.

Instead of saying what she really wanted, she asked, "Would you like some stew?" It was only meant for Wendy, to help her heal, but Felisha had gazed at it with hungry eyes.

"No." Felisha turned around and crinkled her nose before leaving Frankie's view. "I prefer my own cooking, thank you."

Frankie nodded, even though Felisha couldn't see her. Sighing, she picked up a spoon and placed it into the stew. The stairs groaned as she headed up to her shared room with Wendy.

A noise from inside caused Frankie to stop in front of the closed door. Voices radiated from inside. No, not voices, only her sister's. "Will you tell me about your life again?"

Frankie craned her neck so that she was only a millimeter from her cheek touching the door, to get a better listen.

"What do I dream about?" Wendy asked, her voice weak. "Going outside again."

Frankie's chest ached when she heard Wendy's words. It had been weeks since her sister was able to go outdoors. Quietly, Frankie pushed open the door and peered inside. "Talking to ghosts again?"

Wendy wasn't frightened by Frankie's intrusion, just gave a tiny shrug. "Only Gordy."

Frankie smiled a small smile at her younger sister. She'd already heard so much about Gordy and what a gentleman he was. "I remember those days of having imaginary friends."

"Again, Sister, he's not imaginary." Wendy let out a little giggle. "He's standing right beside you."

A chill crawled up Frankie's spine as she slowly turned to the spot where Wendy was looking. Nothing was there. She wanted to slap herself for believing that something could be. "There's no one."

Her sister cocked her head and grinned. "Gordy has a crush on you, you know." Wendy shifted her eyes from Frankie to a spot across the room. "Don't lie, Gordy. You're always asking where my sister is, and you've even mentioned how pretty she is."

Frankie frowned in confusion because Wendy's imagination was becoming a bit too unrealistic. Above her sister's brow, beads of sweat had gathered.

Setting the stew beside Wendy's bedside, Frankie leaned over to press a hand against her sister's head. "You're burning up!" She quickly grabbed the dry rag from the headboard and dabbed at Wendy's forehead.

"I'm fine, Gordy!" Wendy shut her eyelids.

"I'm Frankie." When her sister didn't respond, Frankie wrapped her hands around her sister's shoulders and lightly shook her. "Wendy? Wendy!"

But she didn't open her eyes.

Death should have been a usual occurrence by now, but it was something Frankie would never really get used to. And if she did, maybe she wasn't really human after all. In that moment, she wished she *wasn't* human. The room with the ornate yellow wallpaper, the dresser, and the old writing desk seemed to spin around her.

"Auntie!" she screamed, releasing her sister's shoulders and clasping the headboard.

The dizziness didn't dissipate when she straightened.

Something moved in her periphery. Before she could fully turn to the image, Frankie's legs buckled, and she dropped to the floor. The last thing she heard before she closed her eyes was a man's voice shouting out her name.

Frankie fluttered her eyes open, meeting sunlight for a split second, and then shut them again. Her entire body felt so weak, her muscles stiff, and she wanted to sleep for days. Finally, after many struggling attempts, her eyes opened and settled on a man around her own eighteen years of life. He sat on the edge of her bed, black hair cascading to his shoulders, a lock falling over one blue eye.

"Who are you?" she asked, her throat dry.

"Gordon." His voice had a thick and deep sound

that was pleasant and friendly.

The room was still spinning as she sat up in bed and rubbed her eyes. "A doctor?" Her memories hit her like a hammer to the skull, and she twisted her neck to her sister's bed, throwing off the covers. "Where's Wendy?"

Gordon shook his head, something akin to sorrow crossing his face. "She passed two days ago, and she's already been buried."

Frankie needed air—her lungs were lagging. It couldn't be true. "Where are my aunt and cousin?" They couldn't have just left her for days in this room, making her miss her sister being buried, could they?

He shrugged, but his eyes never left hers.

Frankie stood and noticed she was wearing a white nightgown. Her aunt or cousin must have helped dress her. At that moment, the door flew open and her cousin stepped inside the room.

"Well, since you can't serve yourself, guess who became the next servant?" Felisha spat. "*Me*. That's who." Her cousin flicked her red braid over her shoulder.

"I don't need a servant." Especially if it was to be Felisha.

"You've already ended up like your sisters and are going to die anyway." Pursing her lips, Felisha crossed her arms and leaned on the doorframe.

Frankie's shoulders slumped and she glanced at Gordon, then back at her cousin. "I don't need a doctor. I'm feeling *fine*." She wasn't feeling all right at all, but she didn't want this attention from anyone.

Felisha's brow furrowed and a deep crease formed

down the middle. "The doctor is on his way—we've had it handled. It isn't as if your fever ever got too terribly high, but Mother wants to make sure."

"Thanks, Gordon," Frankie said with a hint that he could leave. "That will be all."

"Who's Gordon?" Felisha took a small step forward. "And who are you talking to?"

Frankie's head twisted to where Gordon was standing, chewing on his lip and staring at the ceiling. He didn't say a single word.

"The man right there!" She pointed fiercely at the guest.

Felisha shook her head with no concern whatsoever. "I think you're starting the hallucinations, same as Wendy did. Remember Gordy? Or have you already forgotten?"

Frankie gripped her skull—she avoided looking at the man that she could still see in her periphery. It wasn't possible. "Take me to Wendy."

"You're too sick and need to rest. Going outside to the cemetery will only make things worse."

"I feel fine!" she lied.

"You'll stay in here before you condemn anyone else. I'm probably already catching whatever is festering inside you." Felisha put her hand on the doorknob. "Now sit down, and I'll bring you your dinner."

Turning around, Felisha's skirts swished as she shut and locked the door. Why were there locks?

Behind her, Frankie could hear light breathing. Shakily, she turned to face the man—Gordon—still seeing him there. She hurried to the door and twisted the knob, but it had indeed been locked. She couldn't leave and she wanted to scream.

Holding her breath, she turned back around, and the person, who only she could see, stood with a blank expression. "Gordon—Gordy?"

Slowly, he nodded and gave a slight bow. "My lady."

"Why-why can I see you? I didn't before." Wendy had really been seeing Gordon all along, but there had to be a reason why she couldn't see him until now.

"Because," he whispered, "you're dying, my lady."

Her entire body stilled, the heart inside her chest seemed to no longer exist as it quieted at the same time. But then it pounded, pounded so fiercely she couldn't keep her breaths even. "It's not lady... My name's Frankie or Francesca, but I prefer Frankie." Her lower lip trembled on the last word.

"I already knew your name... Frankie."

A tiny memory came to her from before she'd passed out and struck the floor. "It was you who I heard before slipping away, wasn't it?"

"Yes, it was."

"Are you dead?"

He nodded.

Her heart beat more frantically than it ever had as she stared at this man, this demon, this ghost. "Only the evil stay. You would have passed when you died."

Gordon nodded again. All the time he'd remained standing beside her bed as if glued to the floor. She got a better look at his face as she focused clearly on it for the first time. High forehead, plump lips, straight nose, and a strong jaw. He was pleasant to look at.

"Are you bewitching us one at a time? Is that it?" she whisper-shouted and backed up until she hit the wall.

A sigh escaped his well-shaped lips as though he was human, as though he was going to put a spell on her with his words. "No. I'm trapped here because of things I've done in my past. Things that I thought were out of my control."

Frankie stared hard at the man in front of her, building up the courage to calm herself down—to stop thinking irrational thoughts. Her bare feet moved over the cool wooden floor. Without taking her gaze from his, she held up her hand, not trusting herself at the moment—or her possible ill-induced hallucinations.

Her eyes stayed locked with his and she spread her fingers apart. "Touch me, then."

For a long time Gordon stared at her before deciding to shuffle toward her. Biting his lip, he pushed his hand forward. Frankie waited for his fingers to pass through hers. But they didn't—his skin, not quite warm, not quite cool, pressed against hers. A squeak escaped her lips, and she yanked her hand away, then bounced back on the bed.

"I can feel you!" Her hands flew to her mouth and she looked away from him.

"Yes…"

"But how?" And even if he was a ghost, or something like that, she'd have expected him to feel as cold as ice.

"I told you before… You're dying." His tone was incredibly soft as if he knew saying anything slightly wrong would cause her to panic. However, she still trembled.

Frankie wanted to scream and cry, but who would she call for? Her ridiculous cousin or her aunt who wouldn't be able to do anything anyway?

"How are you here?" She pulled her knees to her chest and rested her back against the headboard.

A knock at the door interrupted Gordon before he could answer. The door pushed open, admitting Dr. Williams, the same doctor who had treated each of her sick sisters.

"Good day, Miss," Dr. Williams said.

"Good day, Doc."

Dr. Williams was a burly man with large spectacles, a mustache that curled at the ends, and reddened cheeks. He was a kind man, but Frankie wanted him gone. She wanted to be alone, or better yet, wanted her sisters back.

From his bag, the doctor pulled out a stethoscope, motioning her to lean forward. The stethoscope felt cold, even through the fabric of her thin nightgown.

"Take deep breaths," he said.

She did just that, inhaling, exhaling, all while watching Gordon who stared at the door with his hands in his pockets.

"Your heartbeat is a bit sluggish, but your temperature feels fine at the moment." He raked his hand through his side-swept hair. "I know what you're thinking."

"I'm ending up like them, aren't I?" It was what had happened with all her sisters—she knew straight down to her bones what the outcome would be.

"Let's not focus on that. I'm going to leave you

some medicine to try." Before he left, he set the liquid-filled bottle at her bedside.

After he closed the door, she heard the lock turning. She picked up the bottle, inspected the written words, and tossed it against the wall. The medicine hadn't helped any of her siblings anyway.

Gordon took a seat on the floor in the corner of the room where he stayed huddled. She didn't speak to him and he didn't speak to her. Sometimes she could feel his eyes on her, the way hers kept secretly shifting to him. Even when staring elsewhere, she still felt his heavy presence.

No one else came in to check on her—not Felisha, and not her aunt. Frankie gripped her hair and felt the buildup of days spent sweating in bed. She stood from the mattress and padded toward the bathroom that connected to her room.

"Where are you going?" Gordon asked, rising from the floor. His forehead wrinkled as if she would vanish.

"I'm going to rinse off." She thought about something then—a fear that he could walk through walls or *bathroom doors* and do what he wanted. "You aren't going to come in, are you?"

"Not unless you ask me to." She couldn't tell if he was trying to be flirtatious, but his expression remained on the serious side as though she quite possibly might need his help.

"No, thank you, I'll be fine."

Whirling around, Frankie quickly went into the bathroom and shut the door. She undressed and turned on the water, letting the tub fill as she stared at herself in the mirror. When she glanced down at her bare legs, they were covered in blue and purple bruises. Her sisters had started to bruise easily, too.

Her curly brown hair was matted, her lips dry, and her skin pale. Shaking her head, she turned off the faucet of the tub and let her body sink down into the warm water. She scrubbed and scrubbed away at the remains of old sweat and too many thoughts. Tears slipped out then. All of her sisters were gone, and Wendy was the last tether of that siblingship. Now Wendy was dead, too. She closed her eyes and cried harder, until she couldn't anymore.

Time passed as she sat there, while the water grew cold. She released the drain and continued to sit in the tub until her body was covered in goosebumps and she started to shiver.

After she stood, she let out a small groan because she'd forgotten her clothes. On the ivory counter, there was nothing but a bar of soap and a dinky rag. She hadn't refilled the towels, and it looked as if her sister and aunt hadn't either. She also didn't want to use the old sweat-covered nightgown.

"Gordon?" she called, stepping right up to the door, water cascading down from her hair to her feet.

There came a shuffling movement, as if he pushed up on the other side of the door. "Yes?"

"Are you… Are you able to grab things?" Perhaps she wasn't clear enough. "Material things?"

"Mmm hmm."

"Can you pull me out a new nightgown and … undergarments from the dresser." Her cheeks warmed, and she was glad he couldn't see her.

"Of course."

She closed her eyes and silently cursed because she could have asked him to only collect the nightgown. After she'd dressed, she could have gotten the rest later, but it was already too late—the words had been spoken.

With the small rag on the counter, she dried herself off the best she could.

Standing firmly against the door, Frankie pulled it open. Gordon remained there with the clothing, and she hurriedly plucked the things from his hands. A thought entered her mind. "If my cousin had walked in with you holding these, what would she have seen?"

"She'd have seen floating clothing." He smiled. And it was the first time she'd seen him smile that day. It was a beautiful smile, one that easily caused a fluttering in her stomach. Something else came to her then.

"Is it possible you could leave the room and haunt her for the night?" The thought of Felisha squirming over objects moving would help ease things for a little while.

"If you insisted." Gordon's grin grew so wide, he was practically glowing before it fell and turned into another emotion she couldn't name. "I haven't explored the house in years. I used to go to the graveyard, but now I remain here or in the attic."

The stairs to the attic were in the room across the hall. She loved spending her time up there too, writing in her diary. She wondered if he'd been there when she had, but she didn't ask.

"Wouldn't you have to go through the house to leave for the cemetery, though?"

"No." He motioned at the wall. "I can walk right through."

"Oh, yes, being a ghost and all." Realizing she was still talking to him while being unclothed, she moved back and gently shut the door. She stayed near as she dressed and continued, "So, you mentioned years?"

"Yes, it's been a while." He sounded as if his head was right against the door, and something in his tone spoke of a deep sadness.

She'd only been living there with her sisters for the past year. Her aunt had bought the home several years after her husband passed away because she couldn't stay with all the memories at the old house any longer. Frankie didn't know anything about any of the previous owners. But now she was curious and wished she did.

After running her fingers through her wet hair, she pushed open the door to find Gordon already seated on the edge of her bed. It felt improper, but he wasn't even alive so she didn't believe it mattered. Besides, she would probably be dead in the next few weeks or months, and this might be as close to a man as she would ever get.

Before she could sit next to him, the door opened and Felisha plopped down another tray. After scooping up the old one, she hurried and shut the door as if Frankie were a disease.

Frankie had barely touched the first tray of food, but her stomach was starting to tighten with hunger. She picked up the tray with steaming stew, a not-so-red apple, and a glass of water, then brought it to the bed. "Do you eat?"

Gordon shook his head, running his long fingers across the quilt.

"Of course not." The soup scalded her tongue, but she was famished and finished everything in an unwomanly manner. A thin line of the broth slid down her chin, and she swiped the sleeve of her gown across her mouth.

Gordon took the tray from her hands and set it beside the door. Minutes passed and the room started to blur—she could feel her body growing cold. "I'm not feeling so well."

He pressed a hand to her forehead. "You feel okay right now. Do you want me to let you rest?"

She latched onto his sleeve and held him in place as if she was a child losing her prized toy. "Please stay. I don't want to be in here alone without Wendy." As each of her sisters had died, someone had always been in the room, but not anymore.

She closed her eyes then, still grasping the sleeve of a man, who was really a ghost, who was already dead, who was the only person that could be there with her. As she drifted off, dreams consumed her—decaying bodies, blood dripping, and large spiders rolling her in their webs. She sat up, her body shivering from the nightmare.

"I think your fever started again." The gentle voice caused her to jerk forward. For a moment, she'd forgotten about everything, including who he was.

Frankie relaxed back against the headboard and stayed in a sitting position. The silence was becoming unbearable and she couldn't fall back to sleep. She grew inquisitive, wanting to know more about this person who seemed quiet and gentle.

"Gordon, will you tell me about your life?" she asked.

A low chuckle escaped his throat, one that didn't sound happy. "The days bleed into nights and all I have is torturous thoughts." She couldn't imagine what it would be like to continuously sit in this room or an attic. Why did he stop leaving?

"What about your life before?"

"Are you sure you want to hear it?" he asked, as though he was unsure if he wanted to tell it himself. "It's not a pleasant one. There was a time when I was not a good man, in fact, I still am not."

"Don't we all have a bit of the devil in us? We just have to learn to push the creature away." Frankie had always believed in good and bad and sometimes her thoughts turned toward the dark side of things, but she always stayed good.

"That's the thing," Gordon murmured, his voice silky. "I *was* the devil."

Her body froze and she gasped.

Gordon's hand shot out and clasped hers. "Or, to word that better, I gave into temptation."

Her hand grew sweaty, but she didn't rip it away, even as part of her wanted to. Not yet. "Go on."

"I had a fiancée once," Gordon started. "We were to be married, but I caught her making love to my brother."

"Oh no." Her eyes widened. "So you—"

"I killed them," he interrupted.

That was not what she expected him to say, not at all. "I'm…" Frankie didn't know what to say. Was she frightened? She didn't feel scared, but should she?

"That's not all, though, because ... because I liked it." Gordon released her hand as if giving her a chance to run away if she wanted. Yet she stayed. "They weren't the first. My first kill was at fifteen. I had always loved the sight of blood, even though I told myself it wasn't normal. Even though I knew it was wrong. There was just something soothing about seeing it flow. To keep the temptation away, I would cut myself, until something inside me needed more, wanted more. So at fifteen I began taking lives. Sometimes I could fight the urge, and sometimes I couldn't. I'd try to take the older ones since they would be dead soon. But after my fiancée and brother, the craving became worse. I knew the only way to end it was to give up my own life. And what better way than giving myself a fatal wound and watching the blood pour from my veins until I was no more."

A dance with the devil.

Frankie's body remained straight as a board, her breathing too loud. She knew it was wrong to want to do things like that, but apparently so did he. In that moment, she wondered what it would be like to give in to that temptation. What if she snapped her cousin's neck as she'd thought before when she'd been angry?

Quickly, she tucked the thoughts away. "Do you still think about blood now?"

"Every day." He looked away from her, staring up at the ceiling.

Wendy had seen him, as had her other sisters. She thought that they had all been hallucinating, and maybe they had been, maybe she was, too. But for some reason, if she was, she didn't want the image to disappear because she was growing angry. "Did you ever think about spilling blood from my sisters, from *me*?"

Frantically, Gordon shook his head. "Never them. And *especially* never you."

"Now that I can see you... You could hurt me, if you wanted to, couldn't you?"

"I could, but I wouldn't." He paused for a brief moment. "But I could have also hurt you before if I'd really wanted to, up in the attic."

"Because you can still lift objects."

"Because I can lift objects," he murmured.

Something curious in her heart beat at those words, and she didn't say anything. She closed her eyes and rolled over. "I'm tired." But her eyes remained open as she thought about how he had been with her up in the attic. And the sadistic part of her wished she had been able to see him then, too.

For the next four weeks, Frankie lay in bed, regaining strength, losing strength. It was an endless repetition. Her sisters had never lasted this long once they came down with the sickness, but she was *fighting*.

Gordon's image was always there, and by her ability to see him, she knew she wasn't getting any better.

Three times a day, Felisha would hurry and set

down the tray of food and take away the old one. Her cousin stared at her each time as if she wished Frankie was dead. Sometimes Frankie wished she were dead, too, but then Gordon was there to discuss things with.

Since he had talked to her about his past, Gordon remained mum on the subject. His words about spilling blood had been wicked, but somehow she could see past it and wanted to know more.

The door unlocked and opened, and Felisha set down the tray. "I heard you talking to yourself. You're going mad just like your sisters, speaking to things that aren't there," Felisha seethed and slammed the door.

For a long moment, Frankie studied the door and wondered what it would be like to draw a line with a knife across her cousin's throat. But then she shook the thought away. It was only her being angry again, that devil she had to hold at bay.

Gordon placed the tray in Frankie's lap and she brought a spoonful of soup to her mouth. She ate quickly, then drank the bowl full of broth.

After finishing, she set the bowl to the side and her stomach grew queasy. She tried to keep everything down, but she couldn't stop it and all the food came barreling back up into the bowl.

"I'm sorry," she said to Gordon, wiping her mouth with a napkin as she coughed.

Gordon didn't say anything—he peered down with a frown at the bowl and then at Frankie's face. "I think there's something wrong with the food."

"What do you mean?" All she could see was her bile, and her face heated because she'd expelled the contents of her stomach in front of him. She took the tray and set it by the door, but Gordon was already behind her.

"Do you notice you get worse after you eat?" Gordon snapped, yet not at her. "But then when you can't eat for a while, you become slightly better. It seems to be a form of repetition."

"Maybe it's something with my stomach. I prepared all the food myself for Wendy. It can't be that." As she thought about her youngest sister, Wendy had gotten sick, but she had never stopped eating. Some days, Frankie couldn't eat at all.

"You handled all of it?"

She thought long and hard about her movements, cutting carrots, dicing potatoes, preparing the meat. "Yes, everything except for the spices."

"It has to be the spices then," Gordon suggested, rubbing at his chin. "Where do you keep them?"

"In the far back of the cabinet beside the stove."

"Hold on, I'll be right back."

She watched as he walked through the wall and left her alone. A few moments later he slipped back into the room and stuck out his tongue, where she could see a few speckles of the spices resting there.

"I may not eat," he said, "but I can taste the poison saturating the spices."

Her breathing came out heavily, angrily.

The only other two people inside the house were Felisha and Aunt Gemma. And if it really was the spices, then it had to be one of those two people because she wasn't the one poisoning her own sisters.

Felisha refusing the food when Frankie had asked. The insisting that the doctor had said to add the spices.

Her cousin arguing with Gemma about the will and going silent if anyone else entered the room. It was *her*.

"Felisha," Frankie whispered. Something dark slipped into her mind, and she locked eyes with Gordon. "How did you do your first kill?"

"Maybe you shouldn't…"

"Just tell me."

He pulled at his lower lip then blew out a hard breath. "Knife to the throat so the screaming wouldn't come."

Frankie nodded. "Tonight. In her sleep."

When night wrapped around the house in its entirety, she grabbed the knife from the drawer at her bedside. She'd kept it from her evening meal, and she squeezed the cool steel harder.

"The door's locked, you know." Gordon sat down beside her on the bed, his leg brushing hers. "Do you want me to do it for you?"

Closing her eyes, she pictured him with a screwdriver over Felisha's chest, then slamming down a hammer. "No." She'd rather it be her.

"You won't have to worry about regrets or nightmares." He shifted closer until his arm was touching hers. "It would just be one more to add to my stack."

Frankie placed her hand on top of his thigh, right above his knee. "Thank you, but I can do it."

She stood and found a hairpin from the drawer and wiggled it inside the hole of the lock, failing.

"Here, let me help you." Gordon moved behind her, his breath warm at her ear, his cool fingers circling over her hand as if asking her permission.

"All right," she murmured, enjoying the nearness of him a bit too much.

Together, he helped her jimmy the hairpin in until there was a soft click.

"You could have done that this whole time?" Frankie asked, incredulous.

He shrugged. "You never asked."

Secretly, she'd enjoyed spending time in the room with him. It had taken her mind off the death of her sisters, and the company was comforting.

Quietly, she tiptoed down the hall, coming to a stop at Felisha's door. She opened it ever so slowly, her cousin's breaths echoing throughout the room. Gripping the knife, Frankie edged forward until she was standing in the dark, directly above her cousin's bed. Felisha's body was barely lit up by the moonlight, but Frankie could see her head tilted to the side, red hair framing her pillow, exposing her throat.

Frankie's hand quaked, trying to gather her strength, and she clenched the knife harder.

Gordon brushed Frankie's hair aside and whispered in her ear. "You really don't have to do it."

It was as if he was attempting to stop her from being the monster that he thought he was. But if anything, her cousin was the only monster she truly knew. "I do."

"Do you want me to hold your hand again, as we

did with the lock?" He sucked on the edge of his lip as if the thought enticed him. It thrilled her maybe a bit too much.

"Just this once," she murmured.

His hand brushed hers and a rustle of butterflies swarmed in her stomach. Together, they leaned forward and pressed the cool metal against her cousin's throat. Felisha's eyes fluttered open, and Frankie slammed her other hand around her cousin's mouth before a scream could escape. A minor squeak found its way out, and Frankie and Gordon slashed a line on Felisha's skin.

Warm blood met Frankie's hand and she made a twin line at the vein on the other side. With a firm hand, she pressed harder on her cousin's mouth until Felisha's body no longer stirred.

Frankie stared at the blood on her palm, bringing it to her nostrils and taking a long whiff. "Have you ever tasted it?"

"I have," he drawled.

Despite worrying thoughts trying to surface, she pushed them down and brought her hand to her lips, licking the crimson. It tasted salty and full of something else she couldn't name, yet satisfying. Gordon watched her but didn't move, so she held out her hand to him.

"You're a bad influence, you know that?" he murmured. Yet he seemed unable to control himself as he swept his warm tongue against the center of her palm.

Perhaps the wickedness in her had always been there, but hidden deep inside. Perhaps she had only been good for her sisters, and now that they were gone, she could be her true self.

Without a word, as if she hadn't just murdered her cousin, who deserved it after what she'd done, Frankie tiptoed back into her room, more silent than any ghost ever could.

"What are you going to tell your aunt in the morning?" Gordon asked after shutting her door.

"That I killed her." She didn't have an issue confessing to her aunt why she'd killed Felisha. Her cousin deserved it.

"You're braver than I ever was." Gordon was wrong. Maybe he believed himself a coward, but he wasn't. He'd been by her side this entire time.

Her body felt in need of a bath. "I'm going to get cleaned up."

Gordon nodded, their eyes staying locked before he moved his away first.

She had done firsts tonight, and she wanted another first before things came to a close and her aunt shipped her off to a mental institution. But Frankie might die from the poisoning first.

Inside the bathroom, she hurried and washed away the odors of sweat and sickness from her body.

After finishing up and dressing in her nightgown, she opened the door. "Gordon? Could you come here for a moment?"

He glanced up from the journal he was writing in and set it aside to come to her. "Yes?"

"When was the last time you were with a woman?" When she asked him the question, she stared at the floor.

"My fiancée. Why?" His tone was almost curious.

"There weren't any others? Others you had killed?" She'd often wondered over the weeks if he'd seduced women before murdering them.

"No." He shook his head. "It was never like that." Something in his answer made her feel relieved.

Advancing forward, she placed her hand on his chest. The breath in his throat hitched and his lips stayed parted.

"Is it true? What Wendy said?" Frankie asked. "Do you like me?"

Gordon's blue eyes met hers, his expression warm as he softly said, "More than any woman I've ever known. For the past year, your gentleness, your kind words to your sisters, your strength … also your determination. It all drew me in."

Determination with following through with a murder, she thought.

"I had wished a thousand times that you would be able to see me in that attic, if only for moments, but I would never wish for you to suffer like this."

Leaning forward, she let her lips lightly brush his and felt the beauty of his words. Gordon's hands circled around her waist and pulled her closer, but he didn't continue the kiss. Instead, he saved that for her to initiate again, it seemed. So she did.

Her lips caressed his as her hands went to the silver buttons of his shirt. She slid it off his shoulders and lowered her hands to the button of his pants. Not a single word left his mouth—he only kissed her more thoroughly until he was naked and every inch as beautiful as she'd imagined.

"Gordon, I want you to make me feel like a woman tonight." She craved for him to be her first, and she knew he would be her last.

In answer, his hands went to the sides of her nightgown and lifted it over her head. She wore nothing underneath, and a groan, almost feral, escaped his throat. Gordon's fingers caressed and flicked at her nipples, followed by his hands drifting down her stomach and in between her legs.

Her eyes fluttered at the feeling of it all. He turned them both around, and together they fell to the bed.

"Are you sure?" he asked, his hand at her temple.

"More than anything."

Slowly, he pushed inside of her, and she gasped in pain. He paused, and she pulled at his buttocks, letting him know it was all right to continue. After she felt settled and the pain withered away, he thrust inside her. As he moved, she thought about him, and she thought about how easy it was to kill her cousin, the blood, how she would want to do more, do more with him. With each motion between them, Frankie kissed him harder, so hard that if he wasn't a ghost he would have probably been bleeding. She didn't stop because she knew how much he was enjoying it, as was she. Then she cried out from the intense pleasure that erupted, one she never wanted to fade away.

He stayed inside her and pressed his forehead in between the crook of her neck, giving her a soft kiss. And she wished that their life could have been different.

In the morning, a loud sound woke Frankie. She snapped her eyes open, noticing it was the door that had flown open. Her aunt stood there with her hair disheveled.

"What have you done?" Aunt Gemma shouted.

It took a moment for Frankie's eyes to adjust to the light in the room.

Her aunt scanned Frankie up and down. "Where are your clothes, you little heathen?"

Frankie stared down at herself, seeing she was still naked from the night before, spots of blood staining the sheets. Her mouth fell open and she looked to her right, finding Gordon not there. She scrambled to grab her gown from the side of the bed and tossed it on.

Where is he?

"You killed her!" Aunt Gemma ground out, her face a splotchy red, her eyes bulging.

"Felisha was poisoning me!" Her aunt would understand once she knew the truth about Felisha.

"And you"—Gemma pointed harshly at Frankie—"poisoned your sisters."

"Because she filled the spices up with poison!" Frankie's body stilled and she stared hard at her aunt. Something sour was starting to stir in her. "Wait, you knew about it?"

"I wasn't a part of it."

"But you knew about it?" Frankie spat, "And didn't stop it?"

"She didn't want any of you in the will." Anger coursed through Frankie when she thought about how fragile Wendy had become, how Julia cried every day, how Anna became incredibly depressed. Grabbing the knife from the bedside that she'd used the night before, Frankie lunged at her aunt. The blade almost made contact with her aunt's shoulder, but Gemma moved to the side and Frankie tripped, crashing into the wall. Her heart was furious.

Gemma barreled forward, knocking the knife from Frankie's hand. Her aunt plucked it up, and Frankie felt a pain so thick she couldn't think as the blade crashed into her shoulder.

Frankie pulled out the knife just as her aunt turned to go out the door. With adrenaline flowing through her, she jumped to her feet and ran for her aunt. Before her aunt could make it down the hall, Frankie stabbed Gemma in between the shoulder blades and yanked the knife out. Her aunt let out a gasp and a low croak. Then Frankie flipped her aunt around and pierced down from the left to get the blade directly into her heart, if Gemma even had one at all.

Her aunt slumped to the floor, the thump quaking through the house. Frantically, Frankie searched around for Gordon. *Where is he?*

The food. She hadn't eaten for a while and then had thrown up the dinner from the day before. If she was away from the brink of death then she wouldn't be able to see him. *Oh no…*

Frankie thought about her sisters who were all dead. She would surely be put to death for the murder of her cousin and aunt, regardless of what they'd done.

A life here now wouldn't be much of one at all—she wanted the alternative. A wild adventure, filled with a new kind of thrill. And—she wanted Gordon.

Her bare feet stomped against the wooden floor as she ran out the door and headed downstairs. She rushed to the kitchen and ripped open the cabinet, knocking jars out of the way until she found the one with the spices. Opening the lid, she pushed her fingers inside. For a brief moment she hesitated and wondered if she should do it or not—she knew what she wanted.

Frankie ate and ate the tiny pieces of death, the spices dry and bitter as they sailed down her throat. With a glass she filled with water, she swallowed as much as she could. And then waited, and waited, and waited until she thought nothing would happen.

Tired, she pressed her hands against the counter and took deep breath after deep breath. Her head moved side to side and her body crashed to the floor. Everything around her started to become doubled, and tripled, an image sliding in front of her—four Gordons. No, wait, only one. With purple and blue flowers in his hand, he knelt beside her, worried. "You didn't have to do this."

"I wanted—"

Something shook Frankie as if an earthquake was rupturing. She opened her eyelids, meeting Gordon's red-rimmed, blue irises. "I didn't think I'd ever see you again," he whispered.

"I wasn't sure if I'd ever see you." The thought was daunting, but there he was now.

He helped her sit up and pressed a hand to her cheek. "What was it that you wanted before you died?"

"I wanted to see you again—that's why I did it."

A small smile crossed his face. "I'm too bad, and you're too good."

Frankie thought about what happened the day before, what had happened that morning—she wasn't anywhere near good. "You're saying that after last night?"

"No, Frankie," Gordon started, "it was only because of what they had done to you. Revenge makes us do heinous things."

"Maybe. Maybe not." Revenge was why she had done it, but the fact was that she liked doing it more than she should have. The taste of blood in her mouth still lingered.

"I'm sorry I wasn't there when your aunt came in—I should have known there was a possibility that she could have been in on it, too. I had gone to get you flowers." Gordon lifted the purple and blue orchids from the floor and handed them to her.

"Flowers?" she asked, taking the beautiful batch and inhaling the lovely scent.

"Yes…" Was he blushing?

"You may think your heart is bad, but it's good at the same time, too."

"I don't know about that, but if you say so." He smiled. "What do you want to do now?"

"We're leaving this house forever." She wouldn't want to stay there any longer—it was only a reminder of all of the senseless torment and immeasurable suffering that her aunt and cousin had caused to Frankie and her sisters "And if our devilish urges ever prove too strong, I'm sure we can find those who deserve to die for their crimes."

Gordon's lips connected with hers, and she knew with her whole heart that sometimes happily ever afters do come true.

Dearest Clementine,

I had you! I had you in my arms, but Bogdi used a power that I didn't know existed. Your fingertips lingered on mine, holding on as tight as you could, before they slipped away. My fiend of a heart stopped beating for moments and when I opened my eyes, you were gone once more. In the distance, I could hear you shouting my name over and over, yet I couldn't get my body to move. When it finally did, you and Bogdi had vanished. But, my dear, sweet love, you left me a gift again, did you not? You sneaky little minx. A tooth! I think I may know where to go next. Let us both hope that wishes truly can turn into reality. This story reminds me a bit of us, does it not?

Always Yours,
Dorin

Laughter is Always Better
2002

Polli blasted punk music in her car so loud that her eardrums were dancing, ridding herself of the day. The small video store she worked at had basically closed up shop the month before. The porn videos in the back did their duty, but the regular rentals weren't up to par. Customers would rather go to the Blockbuster or Hollywood Video down the street.

Job hunting had been a bitch and nothing had popped up aside from a seasonal position at a Halloween haunted house. Eventually, she'd find something else, but this would have to make do for now. It would only be for a month and a half, but she needed the cash for college because her parents weren't paying for it. She'd already missed the first semester. *Fuck*, she wasn't sure if she wanted to blow her money on it either. Her whole family had gone and were barely making ends meet as it was, and they still had loans up the asshole.

Pulling the car to a stop in front of the large metal fence, Polli shut down her engine and listened to the rest of the fast-paced song, while tapping her fingers against her thighs.

This particular haunted house event was usually held on the other side of town, however, that building had been bought out and turned into a strip mall filled with shitty store after shitty store. Was this what the world was becoming? Chain stores? Nail salons? Cash Advance places? Fuck. That.

Finally she pulled out her keys and threw them into her small leopard purse. The black 1991 Bronco was parked a few spaces down—she'd be working with Evan Dunivan today. There had already been too many years of her dealing with enough of his bullshit at school since Kindergarten. The fucker could never miss a year without being in one of her classes. Right before she graduated, he'd been in three. But even after graduation, here he was.

Even if he was a prick, she liked the Deftones hoodie that he always wore and the way his Dickies sagged, showing a hint of his plaid boxers. She shoved those thoughts away and pressed on.

At the entrance, the padlock was already dangling, so she opened the gate, causing an eerie, horror-movie-sound creaking to take root. Apparently, this Halloween was going to be go big or go home because up ahead rested an old carousel, a rusted playground merry-go-round, and scraps of aged carnival rides spread about. The rides weren't rideable, but they still had the creep factor going on.

The carousel sat covered in chipped-away paint. Some of the horses were scattered around with dismembered body parts and covered in fake blood. Polli didn't scare easily, or at all, when it came to haunted houses, but she thought it was a nice touch.

Behind the tall metal building, the field sprouted high with healthy corn stalks and large green leaves. A narrow dirt path had already been set up the other day, courtesy of Polli and a few of the other workers.

The door to the dark gray building was cracked an inch and her managers, Derek and Lisa, were arguing over the strobe lights. Polli pulled open the door and found them sifting through a box filled with plastic-wrapped tickets and wristbands.

"Hey!" Lisa exclaimed, not lifting her head from the box but somehow knowing it was Polli.

"Polli, my friend"—Derek grinned, his bushy eyebrows rising up his forehead—"I need you to help unpack boxes in the basement with Evan."

"Dammit." Lisa slammed down the roll of unopened tickets. "What kind of plastic is this?"

Polli swiped the roll of tickets to examine the problem. Using the edge of her nail, she poked a loose spot on the side and handed it back.

"I need to figure out a way to stop biting my nails." Lisa huffed, pushing her braids over her shoulder. "We hired a bunch more people to do the acting jobs, so next week we'll be doing a quick rehearsal of things and should be ready to open the house."

"My favorite time of the year." Polli gave a quick fist pump with both fists. All her life she'd loved Halloween, until her mom had told her she was too old for it in the fourth grade. But she'd ignored her mother, because sometimes a child *does* know better.

Polli glanced at the box at the end of the table, brimming with chalky-white makeup and skin crayons. What she really wanted was to be a special effects horror movie artist, but again, not sure if she would be wasting time and throwing her money away.

"Lisa and I have been here all day, and since it's

our anniversary and all, we're about to leave," Derek said. "You think you got it handled?"

"Of course." The good thing about staying busy was the time passed quickly for her.

"Oh, and you know what tonight is, right?" Lisa asked.

Polli rolled her eyes. "I know the urban legend. Supposedly these grounds are haunted and this is the one night of the year that some spirits can rise and blah blah *blah*."

"So be sure to lock up and leave," Lisa said and pinched Polli's cheek. "Can't have anything happen to that cute little face."

Derek let out a groan. "Just ignore Lisa's superstition." He turned to his wife. "And you can't just go around pinching everyone's cheeks."

"I swear, Derek, you try to ruin all my fun." She grinned. "Now back to the strobe light subject."

Polli laughed and let the married couple banter back and forth as she made her way to the basement door. It was located on the other side of the building.

Up ahead, at the end of the hallway, thin strips of white fabric hung from the ceiling to the floor, creating a death gate to what would be the entrance to the haunted house. The fabric looked as if it had been stripped away from a mummy. As she walked by, most of the room was already finished. Exorcist girl in a bed, skeletons dangling from the ceiling, fake blood splattered on walls, and globs of clay that were shaped and molded to look like oozing blobs. There were too many chains and too many zombies. She would've liked a little more vampires and werewolves.

Polli pushed away a thick fabric resembling spiderwebs, and to her left was the basement door, already open. Candescent yellow lighting flooded the room and stairs. The sound of boxes being moved caused her heart to flutter a bit. She ignored that piece of shit heart of hers as she walked down the wooden steps.

At the end of the staircase, opening taped boxes with a razor blade, was Evan. His shaggy blond hair framed his face, and he glanced up when Polli strolled across the room. Hazel eyes met hers and he gave her a smile. She didn't return it.

Inside the room, it smelled like an old library combined with an antique shop. The only décor in the large area was a water heater, an old chair in the corner, and rows and rows of metal shelves. Cans of paint rested on top of one shelf and the rest held boxes.

"There she is," Evan said, softly kicking a box to the side.

"Here I am," Polli replied in a sarcastic tone.

As he bent down and counted out loud, his Dickies shorts started to sag a bit, exposing those checkered boxers of his. This time, they were blue and white. He'd taken off his T-shirt and only had on a white wifebeater. Two black stripes circled around the top of his tube socks, and his Adidas sneakers looked good on him. Even though she hated those shoes with a passion. She couldn't deny the lust-filled thing that happened to her every time she saw him, though.

Brushing past him, Polli picked up a box cutter from the floor and tugged a package toward her.

They worked in silence, pulling costumes out with

holes that reeked of dust. It did, however, give off that much more of a Halloween vibe to the clothing.

Hours went by, and still, neither one of them talked to each other. She spent most of the time putting electronic things together and dressing up dummies. At times, she could feel Evan's eyes on her, and she tried her damned hardest to keep hers off of him.

When Polli looked down at her watch, it was already 9:15 PM. Without so much as a goodbye, she walked up the stairs to leave. She stopped in place when she stared at her only way to exit. The door was shut—she could've sworn she'd left it open when she reached for the knob. It was locked.

Annoyed, Polli yelled down toward Evan, "Did you shut the door and lock it?"

"Did you see me leave this spot?" he said, coming up the stairs to where she stood. "Or are you talking about my spirit floating up there and doing it?"

"I'm not lying," she said, not liking the whiny tone of her voice. "It won't open."

As if he didn't believe her, Evan shook the knob. "Hmm." Backing up a bit, he shot forward and rammed his shoulder against the door.

Polli shot him a look with an arched brow because he'd probably hurt himself. Then there would be nothing he could do about it if they were stuck in the room.

Evan rubbed his shoulder. "It works in the movies."

"Right." She rolled her eyes. "Well, this isn't the movies."

Grabbing at his hair, he headed back down the

stairs. Polli tried rattling the knob one more time and then tossed a lingering stare at the metal door before following him.

"What now?" she asked, searching around the room for an ax, for *something*.

"It looks like we're going to be working overtime tonight." Evan took a seat on the floor and crossed his legs in front of him. She did the same, facing him and not saying a word.

"Why are you like that?" Evan finally asked, his tone implying she wasn't normal.

She was becoming more and more irritated by the second. "Like what?"

"Acting like I'm an abomination or something."

"I do not." She did. Even though she'd wanted him, there had been the fact that he'd been interested in other girls. Girls that weren't her, that wore tight clothes, and giggled over every word that came out of his mouth, including her friends.

"Yeah, right." The tip of his tongue swiped at his lower lip before he softly bit it. "At least twice a day you would give me a dirty look in school."

"That's just my face!" To shut him up, she added, "And you've fucked all my friends."

His brow furrowed as if he was trying to recollect who and what she was talking about. "Are you talking about Angela? That was in the ninth grade, and that hardly qualifies as going past first base." Evan paused and cocked a brow. "What about Aaron?"

Polli tried to keep a poker face. "Aaron doesn't count." He totally counted as her fucking him, and she wasn't going to lie, she'd liked it.

Neither one said anything else, so she stood up and walked to one of the large boxes. She pretended to inspect it, hoping to be left alone, but Evan slithered up behind her.

"I'm serious. I don't get it," he said, his voice soft right beside her. "If you only really knew…" Something in his eyes made it look as though he wanted to tell her more. And, for a moment, something in her made it seem as though she wanted to hear it.

An intoxicating scent of cologne caressed her nostrils, not like the Blue Water shit that Aaron always wore. The fact that she liked the smell of Evan, and how close he was standing, only irritated her more. If anything, she was more annoyed that he'd never chosen her when they were in school. Her stomach dipped when he shifted even closer—she turned around and pushed him up against the wall, caging him in. Evan was taller than her, but all control was hers in that moment. "I don't know, okay? Do you want to just fuck and find out?"

Evan's eyebrows flew up and his jaw dropped. "What?"

"I'm not going to repeat myself." She took a small step back.

He snatched her wrist before she moved farther away, his thumb gently rubbing her skin. "I don't have a condom."

Polli raised a brow and motioned to her purse on the floor. "I have one in my bag."

As if contemplating what choice to make, he chewed on his lip, but then his mouth unexpectedly crashed into hers. His lips were soft and moved hungrily against hers, and Polli's hands automatically went to his face as he drew her closer.

The space between them was growing non-existent, but even the sliver of clothing between them felt like being a mile apart. She pulled on Evan's shirt and while he lifted the rest over his head, her hands were already reaching for the zipper of his shorts. She continued to kiss his perfect lips, all while guiding him to a dusty cloth chair in the corner. One by one, the remainder of their clothing got discarded to the floor.

Despite not wanting to leave for a single moment, Polli snatched a condom from her purse. Wanting to stay in control, she tore it open as she kissed him and rolled the condom on for him, their mouths not once unlocking.

She lowered herself on him, and let the worry of future careers and finding another job fade away with this distraction of a moment. But at the forefront of her mind stayed the boy beneath her. The one she'd wanted to hate so bad. By giving into the lust she'd held for him for years, it all felt better than she could've imagined.

For some reason she wanted to stay watching him and not miss a thing—the curve of his jaw, the slant of his brows, the way he kept swiping his front teeth against his lower lip, the way his eyes stayed closed the entire time she moved.

He came before she did, but that was okay because she felt relaxed. His eyes opened then, and something akin to shame crossed his face. "I'm sorry."

She shook her head because it wasn't a big deal at all. "No, it's all right." If anything, she couldn't believe that this had happened, or how good it had felt.

Evan picked her up out of his lap, as if she was a doll, and placed her on the chair. He went to the wastebasket, discarded the condom, and pulled up his boxers and shorts that were still around his ankles.

"I knew I was going to fuck that up," he said, his voice filled with frustration and maybe a bit of sadness.

"Was I that bad?" Her anger with him was coming back. She wished that she could just not care at times, but she found coating things with anger helped prevent her from falling to pieces.

"No," Evan started. "I was... I haven't... Shit. You know what I'm trying to say."

What the hell is he trying to say? she thought. Then her hand flew to her mouth when she realized his meaning. "You're a *virgin*?" she shouted. "You didn't think to tell me beforehand? And you just lost it in some dusty chair, in a haunted house, with someone you don't even like?"

"Polli, if I didn't like you, I wouldn't have." Evan's tone sounded agitated, but his expression softened.

She couldn't focus right now—she'd been so awful to him, and he'd just... Her heart picked up as she studied him. Taking a deep breath, she scooted closer to him. "Evan, I'm so—"

A loud bang came from upstairs, causing them both to jump. As quickly as she could, she threw on her clothes and dashed to the stairs. Up above, Polli could see the door had flown open.

"Hello?" she asked, grabbing the handrail and walking up.

When no one answered, Evan brushed past her and

stopped at the top. "Who's there?"

Polli slid next to him, seeing only darkness outside the door. Above them, the light bulb flickered, and a shiver crawled up her spine. It almost seemed like a cliché scene in a movie, but something about it felt incredibly *wrong*.

"It's probably just Derek and Lisa messing around. I bet they came back," she finally said, not sure if she believed it herself.

Evan scrunched up his nose at the same time a horrible stench, like fresh manure and rotten eggs, struck her nostrils. "It's possible, but what is that smell?"

She took another deep inhale and covered her nose. "Don't look at me. I don't know what that is."

"It's definitely not you." Evan smiled. "I know how you smell."

Polli didn't have time to wonder about how she smelled to him because he stepped into the darkened hall.

"I think we need to go home," she said, following him out. "It's late anyway."

Neither one had a flashlight as they felt around the building to get to the front. She held onto his wrist, moved the spiderweb-like curtain out of the way, and pulled him along.

"Derek?" Polli called. "Lisa?" There wasn't an answer, only the reeking of death growing stronger and stronger.

"Shit," Evan muttered.

"Are you all right?" She couldn't see anything at all, and the hair on her arms stood on end.

"Yeah, I just hit my leg on something."

She tugged him along because she knew her way out a little better, but she still felt clumsy until, up ahead, lights pierced through the strips of fabric.

When they entered the main hallway, the lights ahead were still on, but flickering like the one in the basement. A crackling sound echoed up and down the hall as if boomeranging back and forth—loud, soft, loud, soft. Her heart increased, drumming, drumming, drumming. No one was sitting at the desk up front. Polli strode with fast steps to the door, only to find it locked.

Something wasn't right, and she wanted to get home. She unlocked the door, opening it to the night sky. A sigh of relief escaped her when she stepped outside into the fresh air. But it wasn't fresh air, the mysterious odor had only increased in strength.

"It's not coming from inside," Evan said, holding a hand over his nose and mouth.

With a shaky hand, she locked the haunted house up as quickly as she could.

"Maybe the urban legend is true?" he suggested.

"Right, just like when I hop in the front of my car, a mysterious person is going to pop up from the back seat and chop off my head." Polli didn't believe in any of that. What she did believe in was that something smelled awful, but it could be coming from one of the chemical plants.

"Morbid. Morbid." Evan took the tip of his finger and tapped it twice against her nose.

"I hate you." The words didn't come out as strongly as she wished them to.

Evan scratched his temple and cocked his head, a smile crossing his lips.

"More than anyone I know," she added for good measure.

"Uh huh."

"Fuck off." He was grating on her nerves, but as she dug in her purse for her keys, she tried to cover up her small smile.

"Why's the gate closed?"

Her head jerked up in the direction straight ahead where he was looking. Derek and Lisa had probably shut it after they left. They both took off on a jog, Evan making it there before her. The latch was closed.

She looked up at the deadly points of the row of singular triangle spikes. "We can climb up and over, just make sure you don't stab yourself at the top."

Polli reached forward, but before she touched the gate, a musical sound drifted through the air from behind her. A fast and high-pitched melody. She whirled to the side, finding the carousel lit up and moving in a circular fashion. That wasn't the part that startled her. No, it was how the broken horses lying on their sides had started to slowly float upward from the ground, arranging themselves in their proper position.

Eyes growing wider second by second, Polli backed up until she hit the iron fence, keys clacking to the ground. An electric current pulsed throughout her body from skin all the way to the marrow buried in her bones. The electricity held her in place as her body shook. It wasn't painful, more like a tingling sensation, but she couldn't move. She wanted to scream, but nothing would pour out from her mouth.

"Polli!" Evan's hand grabbed hers and yanked her away. She expected his body to feel the electricity, but it must've been something ethereal. Her body continued to tremble, whether from aftershock or fright. "Polli!" His hand lightly tapped her cheek, and she took a deep breath.

"Evan, what's going on?" Her tongue felt thick and her body wonky, but she held up her hands and shook them out.

"It's the urban legend," he answered, his voice on edge. "It has to be."

She knew there was an urban legend about a man and woman who'd died, and it was said that every year the couple would find one person each, to take to keep their existence going.

From behind the metal building, bubbly laughter surrounded the field. She froze. Quickly, Evan patted the fence, and Polli expected the same thing to happen to him with the electricity, but it didn't. He climbed up but didn't get far. When he jumped off the top, he appeared back inside the gate.

Polli gasped and Evan's eyes grew incredibly wide. Around the building a heavy thud started—the sound of footsteps.

"Survive the night, and we should be fine," Evan said.

"We're getting out of here." Polli had stopped shaking because she wasn't going to put up with this bullshit from whatever was out there.

The steps drew closer and louder, until out from the side of the building came a woman wearing a billowy black gown, her feet bare. The woman's dark hair was wild and spiked as if she'd run a balloon over it to make the locks stand on end. She appeared hollow, eyes sunken, except there were no eyeballs in her sockets. A laugh came from the woman, her white teeth practically glowing.

Polli's instincts told her to run, but instead, she spotted the keys on the ground and plucked them up—her only line of defense. The woman held out a bony hand.

In between her fingers, Polli felt a slight movement and chalked it up to her imagination. But the feeling came again, a gentle slither across her palm. She peered down and found a long and thick black caterpillar in her hand where her keys should've been. She shook it off, finding her one line of defense gone.

She glanced at Evan, who had an almost entranced look on his face. "Run!" she shouted, tugging him along with her as they sprinted in the opposite direction.

Up ahead, a man already stood there, similar to the woman in the way his eyes were missing. He wore slacks and a button-up, long-sleeved shirt, his hair side-swept, and his feet bare. From behind him came another man and another and another, all laughing and gazing at them with eyes missing. That painful laugh sent tingles throughout Polli's body.

"The other way." Evan yanked Polli to where they had just come from. But she agreed that it would be better to try and pass one of … whatever these people were.

Next to the building, the strange woman had vanished, but in front of the door to the haunted house stood four other laughing women, barefoot and filthy, with their heads bowed. Something latched onto Polli's arm and jerked her to a stop. The woman's bony hand gripped her wrist, and coldness filled Polli, so incredibly cold.

"Let go!" Polli grew frantic, her chest tightening, because she couldn't get out of the woman's release. But all the woman did was laugh with those glowing white teeth of hers. Evan must've somehow noticed because he appeared and tried to tug her away. Finally, she broke free. The woman didn't move an inch, only remained there gazing from those pitiless black holes in her head.

Polli didn't look back as they hurried past the building. Evan's hand took hold of hers, and they increased their pace. Her lungs burned and her thighs ached as they fled.

The cornfield came closer and closer until they reached their destination and came to an abrupt stop. Evan leaned over with his hands above his knees, breathing hard. Polli breathed just as hard as she looked all around for anything that might've followed them. They seemed to be in the clear.

"So we'll run until dawn," Evan said, straightening, still breathing heavily. "Can't be that hard, right?"

"Maybe for you!" Polli whisper-shouted. "I don't know if I can run another two minutes!"

"If I can do it, then you can do it, because I hate running."

Before she could respond, a pulse came from somewhere within her skull. It was as though there was a hand inside, clenching her brain. She let out a half gasp, half cry when the discomfort increased—it then felt as if something was shredding her brain.

"Polli?" Evan edged closer to her, a look of worry appearing on his face.

The desperation on him was making her smile. Her smile got bigger and bigger as his eyebrows furrowed lower and lower until she couldn't control the laughter. It came out high-pitched and shrill—one of the best laughs she'd ever had. It was crazed, like the woman's had been.

Two arms grasped her shoulders and shook her. "Snap out of it!"

Polli couldn't focus on anything except for the laughter, the beautiful sound she wanted to keep making. But Evan wanted her to stop, so maybe she should. Shaking her head as fiercely as she could, she let whatever feelings had washed over her vanish. "Evan, what's going on?"

"Do you think she did something to you?" Evan inspected Polli's face and came to a stop on her wrist.

When she looked down, there rested a thin black line as though a pen had drawn on her. "That's where the woman held me."

"Shit." He rubbed at the spot and added a bit of his spit to try to take it off, but it was as if the line had been tattooed there.

From behind them, a rustling sound reverberated across the field. Cornstalks were being pushed to the side, swaying rapidly. A man stepped forward, the same one that they had first seen after the woman. Polli tugged on Evan, but not quick enough. The man shot forward, enclosing a hand around Evan's throat.

Evan didn't shout or try to leave the man's grip. The eyeless man somehow bore those empty sockets into Evan.

Polli only pulled harder, to no avail. She didn't have her keys anymore, and her nails weren't sharp enough. So she did the only thing she could think of—she leaned forward and slammed her teeth down on the thing's hand. A ticking sound escaped its throat, as if the voice couldn't quite come out.

Snatching Evan's hand, Polli ran with him through the field. It was so big in there, but she didn't know where it would be better to go because strange people kept appearing. They stopped near a large scarecrow—dressed in a plaid shirt, jeans, and suspenders—planted on a post in the middle of the field. Polli knew they weren't lost. If they wanted to get back to the front they'd just have to go in the direction that the scarecrow was facing. With how the world had turned upside down, she expected the scarecrow to hop off its post, but it stood still as ever.

"I felt so cold when that thing was gripping my neck," Evan said softly, shaking a little. "And you bit it…"

For a moment, she remembered the coldness and knew what it felt like. "Yeah."

"For me."

"So?" she ground the words out. It was as though he'd expected her to just leave him there.

"But you said you hated me." He smiled.

"Seriously, go away." Her eyes squinted when she noticed something on his neck. It was a black line that matched the one on her wrist.

The smile on Evan's face spread too wide and a chuckle came out. Light at first, but then it grew louder, enough to irritate Polli. "Evan, you need to chill out."

In reply, his laughter only got more powerful until he collapsed to his knees. Polli had to pull herself together because she wanted to give in to that tinkling laughter. The sound was becoming more beautiful and more alluring by the second. She shook it off to help Evan, but he'd already crawled toward her, his fingertips brushing her leg. His head was bowed and she felt something wet against her leg as he swiped his tongue up it.

Polli shook and her eyes fluttered, but she kicked him away to fight whatever was going on inside her.

She did the one thing she always knew how to do when it came to people, she ran. But after about four seconds, she stopped, stared up at the skies and cursed. Evan hadn't left her behind one single time this night.

Letting out a heavy breath, she slowly turned and took a few steps forward and found Evan, once again, crawling toward her. She knelt beside him and placed her hands on his shoulders, shaking him like he'd done to her, but possibly harder. He only laughed, so she held up a hand and backhanded him across the face.

"Polli." He gazed at her with those hazel eyes and laughed even more, so she smacked him again.

"You feel it, don't you?" she whispered, placing her hand on his reddening cheek. "Inside of you?" Whatever was inside her wanted to join him.

Evan shook his shaggy blond hair, his eyes

fluttering for a moment before fully opening. "I don't know what's going on," he finally said, "but I just wanted to laugh." She knew the feeling, the insidious thing still lingering.

A sound like *tick, tock, tick, tock* filled the air before cackling came from all around her and Evan. Carnival music exploded next to where the carousel was spinning—bright lights flashed in that direction.

Beside Polli, Evan shuddered, and she reached for his hand to prevent her own self from spiraling to somewhere else.

From her periphery, something moved. Polli bit her bottom lip so hard, she could taste blood. It was the scarecrow, pointing in the direction back out of the cornfield, toward the light of the carousel. All of the corn stalks started to move in all directions, and there was nowhere else to run to but ahead. She didn't know whether the hay creation was friend or foe, but she took Evan's hand and together they fled in that direction.

When they broke out from the corn, Polli and Evan continued until they were standing behind the brightly-lit carousel. They both hunched over, taking big and uneven breaths. The night would never end—she knew it in her heart.

Once more, against her temple, came a slithering feeling, as if a snake was flicking its warm tongue across her brain. Polli's eyes glinted, her head nodding back and forth. Evan stared at the carousel, the plastic horses moving up and down—the music seemed to want to pull her away from the insanity.

Instead, she stepped beside Evan and tugged him back. She was desperate to keep him from stepping onto the carousel. So to distract him from leaving, she placed her chin on his shoulder and took a whiff of his neck.

"Polli, not now, I think we need to get on the carousel." Evan grabbed her arms, meeting her gaze, but didn't push her away. Leaning forward, back to his neck, she thought about how she loved the smell of him and swiped her tongue right beneath his earlobe.

"Naughty, naughty, little one," his voice purred, and Polli felt herself slipping more and more into the darkness.

"Where we are headed will be a wondrous thing." Evan's lips spoke the words at the same time Polli's did. And she knew in every vein in her heart that the words they'd spoken were true.

Inside her head, the caterpillars continued to slither, caressing every single one of her thoughts. Something in her screamed to push it all away and go to the carousel, but she wanted to laugh—she wanted to laugh more than anything. With the energy she had left, she thrust it all away, breathing heavily. Evan's arms stayed wrapped around her as he continued to purr like a kitten in her ear.

"Evan, come on!" she said hurriedly, breaking out from his hold.

One of his hands came up as if to claw her, but he began scratching at his wrist, while laughing. Thick red welts formed on his arm, but not deep enough to draw blood.

Polli was becoming more horrified by the second, not knowing what precisely to do. So she grasped his cheeks between her fingertips, her lips a hair's breadth away from his. "Evan, I do like you, okay? I don't hate you, and I'm sorry for everything, but we need to get on the carousel."

His laughter turned to a strange ticking sound, pulsing in his throat. Any other person would've left him and ran. Hell, she was that person to do it to almost anyone, but she couldn't—not after what he admitted to giving up to her in the basement.

A light started to seep up into the sky. Polli released a frustrated sound because she couldn't let him go at it alone. The slithering inside her skull was coming back again, and she glanced to the carousel, which was no longer spinning. The horses were breaking apart and falling to the bottom where they had been before the strangeness of the night began. Polli and Evan were so close, so incredibly close, and she honestly didn't know if getting on the carousel would've helped them or not.

In that moment, Polli couldn't fight anymore. Maybe she should've tried to find another job and never come here at all. Maybe she should've stayed in that dusty basement with Evan.

But she hadn't stayed, and now there was only Evan. Evan and this delicious, devilish laughter. As the full daylight pulled them both under, surrender was all that was left. And so Polli stopped fighting. Closing her eyes, she placed her head against Evan's shoulder, her heart thumping with excitement. She embraced her desire for Evan, a desire that, if she were truly honest with herself, had always been there. Wrapping her arms around his back, she held him tight. It was then that she truly gave in to the laughter and the darkness that promised to erase all of her cares. Polli was giddy to see what lay beyond this place, to find where the beautiful nightmare led. She now knew that sometimes what we always believed we hated is, in the end, what we will always love.

Dearest Clementine,

I found the door and it's sealed. My blood won't work to unseal it, so I need to find someone else who has the right kind to unlock it. There's a mountain not too far away, where a fiend is rumored to live. It will take a bit longer for me to get to you, but your heart is strong. There was a new fierceness in your eyes when I saw you for those brief moments. Please, hold on, and know that I'm coming. Fight that bastard with everything in you because I know you can. You have the courage. You are my little fiend, after all. Your birthday is tomorrow, so this story is a gift to you. I hope you hear it, wherever you are.

Always Yours,
Dorin

Our Hearts Wither Too
1992

*H*is heart was supposed to be hers. She was meant to eat it.

Morgan lay in a bed of rumpled sheets, the dark surrounding her, except for a faint glow coming from a small light plugged into the wall. That tiny spark of light highlighted the man to Morgan's right. A face so delicate when he slept that it appeared to have an almost feminine quality of beauty.

The man's name was Jack, and he was *her* Jack. He rested on his back, fast asleep, unaware that she considered killing him every night as he slept.

They had spent another night together, one of many. Him on top of her, her on top of him, and then her on top of him again, just to show herself that she had a bit more control if she wanted. She knew deep down in her temporary heart that it would be better for them both if she killed him now. One night between them had turned into another, and another, and another. Six months later, here they were. Morgan could feel her control waning with each day they spent together.

Pressing her hand to her naked chest, she felt the heart inside of her beat sluggishly. The time was approaching. Every month Morgan had to find a substitute heart to keep her alive, because each month that particular borrowed organ would die. It was a vicious and repetitive cycle that she chose to continue.

Propping herself up on her elbow, Morgan stared at the outline of Jack's strong jaw, the dark curls that fell around his face, and his high cheekbones. She'd been with men prettier than him, uglier than him, but there was something about his heart, *him,* that prevented her from slicing open his chest to retrieve it.

Jack was different than the others—he was kind and understanding and didn't try to tame her. She liked the way he would grin like an excited child when he watched his favorite movies, the adorable way he would move his lips along with the dialogue, so completely immersed in everything he enjoyed. So completely alive.

I should do it, she thought. *Do it now. End this suffering.*

Sighing, Morgan leaned forward, so that she hovered over Jack. She pushed the silver ring with a pointed end—around her index finger—forward, so the sharp edge would make a clean cut. Gently, she ran it up and down his chest, stroking, prolonging, her hand shaking more and more. Her finger came to an abrupt stop directly over his heart, and her gaze slid up to Jack's face. He was awake, peering down at her with a tired smile.

"You just can't get enough of me, can you?" The light hid his gray eyes, but she knew they were shining with an emotion that she recognized had been growing more and more within him.

Biting the edge of her lip, Morgan warred with herself, but she ended up giving in to her weakness. Him. "No, I don't think I can." Her mouth pressed against his while she pushed her ring back down to the base of her finger. With teasing motions, she slid her hand up Jack's thigh to the place that would make his smile grow wider.

His strong arms wrapped around her, pulling her close. In the back of her mind, Morgan still wanted to know what his heart tasted like, but more than that, she wanted to keep tasting him, relishing him, and feeling his mouth against hers.

In the morning, Morgan left early, gifting Jack a kiss and a goodbye. Her heart was already withering in her chest. She could feel the pumping of the vital organ growing weaker and weaker.

She wasn't human, but she wasn't an immortal either. One day she would die like anyone else. Morgan aged just as humans did, but without a new heart each month to keep her alive, she would die.

As she walked into the early morning, the sun rising into the sky, she remembered the first heart she'd ever eaten. She had been only three years old. It was when her jaw was able to first unhinge so the organ would be able to fit into her mouth and slide down her throat. That first taste—she remembered even now, the deliciousness of it. Before that, her mother had fed her blood from a heart. But at age three was when her first heart had begun to die, and Morgan would not have been able to live if she had kept it.

Now, she would need to get a new heart tonight, or die.

After a long day at work, Morgan was about to leave her art supply store, when the store phone rang. With a sigh, she reached for it. "La Porte Art Supply."

"Are you coming over tonight?" a voice practically purred. "I have something special planned." *Jack.*

She couldn't contain her smile, but then her chest released a small ache, reminding her of what had to be done. "I can't."

"I think you'll really, really like it," he taunted, and she could feel him smiling through the phone.

"If it involves a bath filled with bubbles, I probably would." The last time they had both impatiently ended up in the bathtub—clothes and all.

"It does."

"I can't," Morgan groaned and then told a lie, "I have so much overload from work that I have to go over it tonight."

"Damn. Tomorrow?"

"Tomorrow." Any other day would mostly be normal, especially after her new heart was fresh.

"Morgan?"

She smiled. "Yeah?"

"I love you."

Her smile faded, and she stayed silent on the phone for a second too long before finally rushing out the words, "Okay, bye." She slammed down the phone and stepped away as if it had burned her hand. She knew he was going to say those words, had wanted to say them. Maybe he'd been waiting for her to say them first, but she couldn't.

Jack was twenty-nine, a dentist who used to be a punk rocker, who thought he had officially become part of society. However, he still had that dangerous side that Morgan liked, all while still being able to help make patients' teeth nice and shiny.

She couldn't think about Jack right now as she stepped out of her car. She needed to focus. Her hand gripped the front of her collared shirt, her heart growing quieter and quieter. She had questioned herself numerous times about giving in to her own funeral by not eating a heart, but she didn't want to die. The risk of her ending a person's life in order for her to live a bit longer had never bothered her before. Except when it came to Jack. He'd unlocked something inside her that she wanted to lock back up.

With growing fury, Morgan unclenched her shirt, shook her head, and hurried inside her house. The place was a clusterfuck. Magazine clippings were sprawled everywhere, clean clothing thrown in clumps on the leather couch, and paint bottles messily arranged on the coffee table.

Morgan wasn't an artist by any means, but she

enjoyed taking her frustration out on canvases. Most were covered in red paint because that was the fiber of her being, the symbolic color of blood that a heart pumped to provide life.

"Why can't I be normal?" she whispered. "But normal is something you should never wish to be, Morgan." Her mother used to tell her that when she was a child, and she still held onto it.

Plucking up an open magazine from the carpet, she headed into the kitchen to make herself a sandwich. She flipped through the tattoo magazine until she found a picture that she wanted to sketch. The image was of a shriveled, dried-up heart, like the one inside her chest was becoming.

After Morgan ate and finished painting, she stared at the misshapen heart and took a deep breath. An intense pain struck the inside of her chest and she let out a deep cough that only made it hurt worse. It was already getting harder for Morgan to breathe, and she had to get a heart tonight. The darkness already blanketed her home, so she headed out into the night to do what she must.

Outside the night club, the music was booming as she stepped out of the cab. A few girls in short dresses and high heels entered the charcoal-bricked building. She handed the cab driver a twenty and scrambled out of the car, shutting the door.

Morgan preferred to find someone with a strong heartbeat, someone whom she knew nothing about. Picking up someone at the hospital on their deathbed just wouldn't do. The last time she'd done that, she'd felt sick for the entire month.

A cloud of smoke enveloped her when she walked up the steps, and she swatted at the air. All around her, almost everyone was drinking, dancing, or both. There wasn't time to wait for someone to approach her—she found the first person she could, sitting alone.

The man was tall, thin, almost skeletal. He sipped on a beer and ran a hand through his spiky, chestnut-colored hair.

She adjusted her silky black gloves and placed a hand to the wall and whispered in his ear, "You wanna leave this joint and go to your place?"

His brown eyes slid to hers, his lips curling into a smirk. "Straight to the point?"

Pushing herself away from the wall, Morgan shrugged and backed up. "Take it or leave it."

Despite his eyebrows shooting up in a surprised expression, he quickly followed her out of the club. They both stayed silent as he walked her to his car. The stranger even opened the door for her, as if to prove himself a gentleman when in fact Morgan didn't care either way.

After starting the car, the man put on a country song, and she hated it. Hated the guy's twangy voice and hated being in this car with this strange man. She was glad he didn't offer his name, and she didn't care to ask it. Maybe she should just start slashing people in back alleys. It would be easier that way.

The man, who wasn't Jack, pulled to a stop on a cracked driveway in front of a cozy house on pier and beams. It was cute and blue with a porch swing hanging in front of where a garage had once been.

As they approached the front door with a rectangular window covered in thin metal blinds, her already slowing heart felt as if it was speeding up. She thought about Jack, what she was doing, and it all felt wrong. So she had to do it fast, but the man beat her to the punch. He opened the door and before she could make a move, he pushed her up against it.

His hand cupped her breast, squeezing hard. "Are you going to tell me your name or do I just call you whatever I want?" Before she could answer, his wet lips pressed to hers. They moved sloppily against her, and the feel of them was nothing like Jack's. She wanted him to stop. Instead of pushing him away, she fished out the blade from her coat pocket and steadily buried it into his chest. Then to end his and her suffering, she hastily slashed a smile across his throat. Crimson bloomed out from the wounds and quietly spread. The only sound inside the house was his gasps and slowing breaths.

Morgan still didn't know his name as he slumped to the floor. And it didn't matter. It wouldn't ever serve a purpose anyway.

With a deep swallow, she fumbled with the buttons of the man's dress shirt until his hairy chest sat on display. Taking the knife once more, she sliced a jagged line down the center of his chest, the squishy sounds echoing through the room.

Shifting forward, she pushed at an angle with her

gloved hands inside the dead chest and dug through organs, muscle, and nerve endings until she reached the precious treasure she needed. Blood oozed down her arm as she held the object in her fist.

Breathing softly, Morgan opened her jaw wide, and then wider, and wider, until it became perfectly unhinged. She placed the heart on her tongue and shoved it inside her mouth to the back of her throat, where the esophagus expanded for the new object. The withered one, that had almost stopped beating, was being pushed and replaced by the new organ. As the old heart entered her stomach, the new one took shape inside her chest, growing stronger.

Thump-thump. Thump-thump.

Pressing a bloody gloved-hand to her chest, she let herself relax. "One month. Another month of freedom." As she stared at the dead body, no remorse consumed her. Maybe she was a monster, but she was still alive.

Without a single glance back, she tucked her gloves into her coat pocket and walked home, still covered in blood. If someone stopped her, she would say it was for a horror movie project.

Thirty minutes later, Morgan arrived home and stopped in her tracks when she found someone sitting on her porch. Jack. Maybe she should have washed off.

Underneath the soft glow of her porch light, his gray eyes met hers. Box of chocolates in hand, he stood and scanned her over, really seeing her.

The chocolates dropped from his grasp, and he rushed to her like she was dying, his hands wrapping around her shoulders. "Are you all right?"

She didn't nod or shake her head, only stared at him. Something... Something was happening inside her, and she didn't know what exactly. An emotion she didn't wish to have, one she wanted to slide back inside the heart that had died.

"Did someone do something to you?" He shifted back from her, hands still folded on her shoulders, his eyes almost too intense for her. "Where are you bleeding from?"

"It's ... it's ... not mine," she murmured. A small piece of her wanted to pull the words back, but most of her yearned to tell him everything.

"*What?*" Jack's brow furrowed in confusion, but his hands never left her.

Finally, she moved from his grasp and inched toward the porch, aching to get inside as though this wasn't happening. "Why are you here?"

"Is that the question you're going to ask when there's blood all over you?" He hurried in front of her, up the porch steps, his face incredulous.

She pulled out the keys from her purse and unlocked the door. "Yes."

"I came here to surprise you. I thought I'd bring you dinner."

Her eyes fell to the bag beside the front door. It was Chinese food from her favorite restaurant. Her heart beat as if reminding her what was going on. "I said I'd see you tomorrow."

"Is this because of what I said earlier?"

Those three words he'd said earlier—the ones she'd tried to pretend had never happened—popped into her mind. "Jesus, Jack, just go home."

"What the fuck is going on?" he asked, appearing hurt. It only infuriated her.

"I ate someone's heart."

"What?"

She stared at his confused face and took a step toward him and pressed her hand against her chest. "I. Ate. Someone's. Heart."

"Like a candy heart?"

"No, not fucking candy!"

Jack took a step back and shook his head, running a hand through his curls. "I'm so confused."

Morgan hadn't planned on telling him. Hadn't planned on *ever* telling him or anyone. She wasn't sure what she would have done. Maybe eventually she would have stopped answering his phone calls, or maybe she would have given in to eating his heart. But now, maybe he would have a chance to stay away from her if he knew the truth.

"Follow me inside."

He didn't hesitate and walked behind her into the house. She flipped on the light and he took a seat on her leather sofa, setting some of the mess to the side.

"Well?"

"Can I take a shower first?" She was avoiding answering him for the moment, but if she was going to see Jack one last time, she wanted to feel clean.

"Sure… Go take a shower after you just told me you ate someone's heart and have blood all over you. This is all perfectly normal." His tone was still light.

"Great, you're a peach!" she said sarcastically sweet, turned around, and hurried down the hall.

"Yeah, a peach is something normal you eat!" He

yelled as if everything she had said earlier had never been true.

But it was. The blood crusted on her skin told her that. She rushed through her hot shower, ignoring the fact that Jack was there. Or maybe once she came out, he wouldn't be, and she could finally move on with what was left of her life. But no, there he was, seated on the couch, flipping through one of her tattoo magazines.

He set the magazine to the side when he noticed she was there, but not before she glanced at the paper underneath.

"What is that?"

Morgan reached for the sheet of paper but not before Jack ripped it away. "Nothing."

"Jack," she said his name through gritted teeth.

"Fine." He handed her the folded paper. "I was just writing down all things paranormal."

The paper made a swishing noise as she unfolded it. *Poltergeist*. Lifting her head, she stared at the ceiling and let out a small laugh. She pressed a clean hand against his shoulder. "I can touch you, so I'm not a ghost."

"No, you're definitely not that."

"The blood's gone." She shuffled forward.

"So it is."

The air was already growing heated between them and before Morgan let herself slip into the moment, she blurted, "I have to eat hearts to live. And no, I'm not immortal—I'm not any of that. I don't know what I am. But each month my heart withers, and if I don't eat a new one, I'll die."

Jack blinked and blinked and blinked. "Animal hearts?"

"Jack!" Morgan shouted. "I've been *murdering* people!"

"To live."

"Yes!"

"But not me."

She could lie to him and tell him that she never planned on taking his heart from his chest, but she couldn't do it. Her eyes darted to the side.

"Okay," Jack drawled, "should have been me..."

"But I couldn't..." she whispered, not taking her eyes away from his.

"Because?"

"I don't know!" she shouted again. "Because I like you, all right?"

"So once a month..." He rubbed his hand across his chin over and over again.

"Can you be more elaborate?" she asked, growing antsy and irritated while waiting for him to go on.

"Show me then," Jack said. "Next month when you have to do it all over again. Show me."

"*What?* Why aren't you acting like a normal person? Anyone else would have called the police. Ran off screaming. Tried to kill me." She took a step away from him. "Frankly, you're freaking me out."

"Oh, I'm kind of in shock right now. Once the wheels start really turning in my head, I'm sure I'll panic for a bit."

"If you really want to see it, then come back in a month. If you choose to not show up, I understand."

His eyebrows lowered. "What do you mean a

month?"

"I think—I think we shouldn't see each other. You obviously need some time to process that I'm a murderer or that you think I'm crazy." Morgan attempted to yank Jack from the couch, but he didn't budge. He gave her a tug and pulled her toward him.

"You're just trying to break up with me, aren't you? I don't believe any of this, and I like crazy." He hauled her into his lap and she let out a low moan. He gently tugged down the robe from her shoulders until her breasts were exposed. Morgan knew it was fucked up, but it all felt so good when his mouth enveloped her nipple. She brought her lips to his and almost gave in to the moment before hopping from his lap and straightening her robe.

"Leave, and come back in a month," she said, her tone giving no room for argument.

"Fine. I'll play this game with you, only because I love you." There those words were again. Jack's lips softly brushed against hers, and then he walked out the door.

"I don't love you," she whispered to the door. "I can't love anyone."

Every day Morgan received a letter in the mail from Jack with the three words written inside. She didn't reply. Only pressed her hand to her heart. But was it really her heart if it was stolen? She still wasn't sorry she took the organ, but it made her wonder if any of the victims she'd murdered could have been like Jack. If she'd only killed Jack to begin with, he would have just been an afterthought, but because of her mistake, he consumed her dreams night after night. Perhaps he was an obsession, but it was more than that … she missed him.

The heart in her chest ached, reminding her that it had been a month, and was on its way to disintegrate. It was time. Her breath caught when the doorbell rang.

Padding her bare feet across the living room, she stood on her tiptoes and peered out the peephole. But she had known who it was. Jack's curly head was bowed down, his eyes staring at the ground.

Morgan opened the door and her gaze fell to the chocolates in his hand. He always had chocolates for her, and she would give him nothing but heartbreak.

Jack bit his lip, appearing nervous. "I've missed you."

"Yeah." She missed him more than anything ever but still held her feelings back. "Ready?"

"You're still on this game?" he said, showing a bit of frustration.

Reaching forward, she yanked his hand to her chest. "Feel that?"

His brows furrowed. "Do you need to go to the hospital?"

"No, I told you I need to eat a heart," she said, frustrated, too. "Unless you want it to be yours, I've got to leave."

"Um, just tell me what we need to do."

The fact that he said *we* triggered something

because she didn't need anyone else to help her. Yet she took a seat inside his car and folded her hands in her lap, twiddling her thumbs to calm down her thoughts.

"Where to?" he asked, gripping the steering wheel tightly.

She wanted somewhere less busy. "The bar on Main Street."

He nodded, and they drove in silence. There was so much she wanted to say to him, but she would only become weaker the more she talked.

Jack pulled onto the street and Morgan had him park on the side next to the curb.

"Now what?" he asked.

"Now you'll see the rest," Morgan responded while slipping on a new pair of silky black gloves. She then handed him a pair of leather ones and headed for the bar.

Outside the bar stood a man with tan skin and thick obsidian hair, flipping through his wallet.

Morgan stopped in front of the man. "You want to come back to my place?" She knew with her whole decaying heart that Jack had his fists clenched at his sides and his eyes wide. It made her smile.

The man's gaze drifted from her to Jack. "I'm not down for threesomes."

"He'll only be watching," she purred.

"Nah, that's all right," he drawled in a deep southern accent.

Before the man could turn around to leave, she kneed him between the legs and punched him in the face. The man slumped to the ground.

Jack tugged her backward. "What the fuck are you doing?"

"I don't know what I'm doing either, but I'm dying, Jack. Fuck it, I—I love you, but I don't have time for this," she seethed.

Jack's eyes shifted from the front door, to her, to the man on the ground who was regaining consciousness. "So help me I'm going to go to jail for you, aren't I?" He knelt and slammed his gloved fist into the man's face, knocking him out. With hurried movements, Jack dragged the body around the building. The reek of garbage coming from the trash permeated the air of the alley.

"What now?" he grunted, sweat beading his brows and forehead.

Morgan withdrew her knife and flicked it open to draw her two-hundred-and-forty-second smile at the man's throat, the quickest way for him to not wake again.

A pain so harsh struck her heart and she dropped to her knees, her shaky hand clasping her chest. The knife fell to the ground with a clack.

Jack grabbed the knife, and she feared for a moment that he was going to haul her away. But he moved forward and put the smile on the throat of the man for her as if he'd done it a thousand times before.

"You—you—" she stuttered, her eyes frantically shifting back and forth.

"Now what do you need?" he whisper-shouted.

"His heart." She crawled forward and attempted to unbutton the man's shirt. Her fingers kept fumbling as she grew weaker. Jack's hands softly brushed hers away and he opened up the shirt, popping off a few buttons.

Stabbing the blade into the man's chest, Jack created a long uneven incision. His shoulders didn't shake as he rolled up his sleeves and reached inside the flesh, digging around until he found the very thing that Morgan needed to survive. Jack's eyes met hers when he pulled out the organ and cradled it in his palms. She couldn't read his thoughts, and she wasn't sure she wanted to, either.

The smell of metal caressed her nostrils and she opened her mouth wide, letting her jaw unhinge.

"Holy shit!" Jack whispered, his hand trembling for the first time when he gave her the bloody heart. Without taking her gaze away from his, she scooped up the organ from him and placed it into her mouth, swallowing the muscular heart whole. Her throat expanded as the heart slid down, replacing the one that barely had any breaths left.

When the fresh organ beat rapidly in her chest, and she felt back to being whole, her eyes met Jack's again. "I don't know what I am."

"You're Morgan," he breathed, his hands no longer shaking.

She looked at the dead body on the ground and the voices from outside, just on the other side of the building. "We have to leave."

They hurried around the opposite side and didn't stop until they were in Jack's car. Once inside, they removed their gloves.

As Jack started the car and drove away, Morgan used a rag and wet hand wipes from her purse to remove the blood from her face. The same as on the ride to the bar, they remained quiet, but this time for a different reason.

When Jack parked in front of her house, he turned to her, worry shrouding his face. "That's how you've been doing this? All these years? Reckless?"

"Yes…" It was the fastest way that she knew how to do things. Go in for the heart, and quickly leave with it.

"We're going to have to be more careful and figure out a better plan," Jack said gently. "I mean, that was too risky."

"We?" Her new heart beat a happy rhythm at the words, and she wanted to shove it away because she could do the tasks alone. But … there was that *but* lingering within her.

"Did you mean what you said back there?"

"That I love you?" Something about saying those words felt easier now.

"Yeah?" She didn't want to deny how she felt any longer.

"Well, we're both in this too deep now, so I guess we're in this together, right?" His arms were still splattered in dried blood as he pressed his palm to her cheek, but she didn't care.

"This is my problem, Jack. I can find the hearts I need without your help. I've been doing it alone for years..." Morgan paused, worrying her lip in between her teeth. "But if you insist..." She leaned forward and pressed her forehead to his before softly kissing his lips. She had been alone in this for so long and now she wasn't. It all felt so strange, but possibly right at the same time. She knew if she was fully human that all this murdering would be wrong, but she was something else. This was her survival, just as a vampire needed blood, and now she wanted more than anything to keep on living with Jack.

"Let's get cleaned up, and I'll tell you everything," she said, letting her new heart fill up, for the first time, with love. "It's been a month since I've seen you and I'm going to prove each and every day this month how much I missed you."

"If you insist," he echoed her earlier words and smiled.

Dearest Clementine,

I haven't gotten to the mountain yet, but I should be able to make it by tomorrow. If all goes well, I'll have the blood to unlock the door, and I will find you. That is, if she gives it to me willingly. I've never been forceful, but I'll do what I must for you, my dearest. I'm going to be honest here, this is the one time I've felt truly lost. My thoughts are starting to become "what ifs." I'm holding onto the memory of that perfect moment when you put your hand against my cheek and asked me to marry you. Of course I said yes. While I hold onto the good times, this is the next tale I have for you.

Always Yours,
Dorin

Sometimes We're Not Hungry
2032

A pounding reverberated against the outside walls, repeating over and over. The screams grew more horrible with each passing second, as though they would never end. They tore at Siri's nerves until she thought she would go mad with the suffering around her. Suffering she could neither stop nor run away from.

In a stranger's room, on the second floor of an abandoned apartment, Siri closed her eyes. She'd been there for three days, confined, waiting for Camille to return.

She hadn't.

It should've only taken one day to go and check for an escape. One. Day.

Siri moved the dusty curtains back from the sliding glass door. "Yep, there they are," she said to herself as she gazed out. There were others—like her—hidden in rooms in the old building, remaining out of sight, yet the live ones outside had an uncanny ability to find them.

She had waited long enough.

Siri had promised Camille she wouldn't try and go after her no matter what, but she wouldn't listen this time.

Alice released a soft purr from behind her. Siri

turned around to face Camille's kitten. "You know I only stayed here to watch you because she's obsessed with having you *not* die."

Alice lifted a tiny paw to her mouth and gave it a soft lick, ignoring Siri.

She hated that damn cat, but she loved Camille so she accepted the feline.

Camille had been gone for three days. 892 days since Siri had been dead. 742 days since Camille had died. An outbreak had ripped the world to shreds. Her parents gone, her siblings gone, her dog gone, her old life—all of it—was *gone*.

The thing was, Siri's parents had been eccentric. One of those apocalyptic fanatics seen on the news. They'd had a basement filled with canned *everything* and also batteries, flashlights, inflatable mattresses, board games, you name it. Her life had been insanity growing up. But when the outbreak came, she was the only one in her family left.

Infection, they called it. Movies always called it that, too.

Yet, this infection didn't spread through saliva or bites. It had been airborne. And then people died. Lots of people. But then the ones who died came back— pale and never hungry. And the ones who didn't die? Well, they became something else entirely. They became "The Ravenous" or "Ravs" for short.

Siri stared at her pale hands—she was the once dead or now undead. Zombie could be considered the right term but she didn't hunt down flesh to eat. No, that pastime was for the Ravs who preferred that adventurous activity.

A howling scream echoed from outside, signaling the Ravs—who she preferred to think were more like vicious beasts—were increasing in number.

"And guess what, Alice." Siri looked at the cat—not an undead. "We may need to leave before I become their dinner. What do you say ol' girl? Ready to head out?"

Alice placed her paw down and stared up at Siri, unimpressed. The feline either didn't understand Siri or just pretended. She would go with pretended.

Siri never understood why the ones who died and came back weren't the attackers. The Ravs had this addiction to wanting to eat undead flesh. Dead skin, muscle, and blood didn't seem appetizing to her in the slightest. But since she'd died, eating anything wasn't important anymore. She just roamed around with her pale skin, dark circles under her eyes, and constantly ran from Ravs. In this world, one would think the undead attacking humans would be the norm, but nope.

As she parted the curtain again, a few of the Ravs, with hunger etched in their faces, charged at one of the doors. To her right, Siri caught something moving.

"Oh, look, Alice, one already has something in its hand." She turned to the cat and called her over. She didn't come. "It looks like a leg." Blood was sprayed all over the pavement. *Seems more undead didn't make it.* She sighed and did a silent prayer, hoping the remainder of the body made it off somewhere.

She missed the hunger at times. Missed the taste of food. Anything. But at that moment, she was ecstatic to be what she was. Having a leg in both her hands didn't seem like the bee's knees.

Closing the curtains, she turned to Alice again. "Get ready, girl, we're going out to find Camille." At the sound of Siri's girlfriend's name, the cat perked up. "Figures." She rolled her eyes and tore off the borrowed clothing.

Siri pulled back on her plaid mini skirt, tank top, black leather jacket, and slid on her Doc Martens boots. She didn't care that she was in some real-life apocalypse, she was still going to look good.

"Where's my baby at?" Siri said, looking around the room. "No, not you, Alice." She finally spotted the machete strewn on the carpet on the other side of the room. "There it is."

Siri lifted the beautiful weapon from the stained floor and took a deep breath. She was going to go search for Camille. If something happened to her girlfriend, she'd kill everyone involved, no matter the headcount.

She still missed the firearms, but she ran out of that a long time ago. But she still had her skills in hand-to-hand-combat training that her dad taught her during childhood.

Scooping up her backpack from the floor, she opened it on the bed beside Alice. "Get in."

The cat didn't move.

"Get in or stay here."

Alice glanced away from her.

"Fucking cat." She picked up the feline and placed her in the backpack. The cat yowled, but Siri couldn't carry her and use the machete if she needed to. This huge sacrifice of not leaving the cat behind was all for Camille. That was true love right there.

As quietly as she could, Siri slid open the glass door. She looked back at the room, knowing it was better to do this than become a cat lady. A life alone with Alice, if Camille never returned, wasn't her idea of a good time.

When she stepped out, no hungry Ravs looked her way. She hunched down, so the patio walls covered her body, and took several deep breaths. "Alice, you better stay quiet." For the first time in her feline life, the cat listened.

With steady hands, she placed her palms on the wall and peered over. The surrounding buildings were all crumbling with broken windows. And the Ravs seemed to be all gone. But then she spotted movement just as a scream ripped through the air. *Oh no, wait, there they are, in all their murderous glory.*

Thankfully, they were farther back near the garbage bin. Despite knowing she could be eaten, Siri placed her hands on top of the wall and skillfully leaped over it. The descent was a short fall, and her shins rattled with the heavy landing, but she felt good.

A Rav with dark spiky hair lunged after her. Instead of darting away, she ran after him and swung her weapon—the head landed on the ground with a sickening thump-thump. Siri smirked at her win and sprinted toward the empty street.

Two Ravs hopped out of a car and barreled toward her, saliva streaming down their chins in hunger. As film had depicted, neither the undead nor the living moved at a too slow or too quick speed—that part of life remained happily the same. However, movies had it right about the extreme hunger—minus it being dead things doing the deed.

Using the machete again with perfect precision, Siri struck one woman with red hair through the neck, and a gurgling sound poured from her mouth as she plummeted to the ground. Pulling the weapon out of the corpse, she drove it through the other Rav's heart, the way Camille loved to.

Up ahead, the roar of an engine erupted through the air. Siri held the machete higher and got ready—Alice softly moved around in the backpack. Siri looked over her shoulder, not seeing anyone else on this side of the building, but she could hear stuff going down on the other side, judging by all the screaming and groaning.

As the car drew closer, she spotted bright pink hair through the windshield and she almost dropped the weapon. Almost.

Camille rolled the car to a stop with the window down as if it was a normal day. "Sorry I'm late, but look what I found." She held up a sheet of wrinkled paper with a bunch of mumbo jumbo written on it.

"I thought you were dead!" Siri raced to the car, yanked open the door, and hopped inside. She turned the backpack around and unzipped it to let the little heathen get fresh air.

When she got a closer look at her girlfriend's face, she noticed it was covered in bruises, and a few bite marks decorated her neck and left arm. Even her skin appeared paler than usual.

"You're hurt!" Siri shouted, grabbing Camille's arm.

"My skin's still intact, so I'm okay. Just a little setback for a couple days that slowed me down."

Camille cocked her head and shrugged. Her eyebrows furrowed and she leaned closer to the steering wheel. "Looks like we've got company." She slammed on the gas pedal, throwing Siri and Alice back against the seat.

After Siri's eyes adjusted, she glanced out the windshield. Three Ravs ran after them, their legs pumping, arms flailing. The car picked up speed. Camille smashed into them like they were nothing. Siri felt the bump as it ran over one's skull.

Siri let out a sigh of relief and picked up Alice, placing her in the backseat. "We were coming after you."

"Ah, my hero." Camille chuckled. "But I told you to wait for me."

"Don't change the subject." Siri narrowed her eyes. "I would've been left with the cat if something happened to you."

"Well, it didn't." Camille smiled broader and pointed at the sheet of paper now on the dashboard. "This here is a map to some abandoned boats."

"Boats?"

"You want to go for a ride?" Camille tapped the steering wheel. "We don't have to worry about eating, so the sea life seems like the life for me."

"Like, become pirates?" The idea was perfect. She should've come up with it herself a long time ago. "I'm in. I may even chip in and gather fish for Alice."

"This is why I love you, darling." Camille quickly jerked the car to the left, striking down another undead-flesh-hungry Rav. "Sorry, had to do it, reminds me of zombie video games. I miss those days."

"I'll keep a lookout for more to strike on the way." Siri rolled her eyes and grinned. Maybe for a while, she could find some peace in the middle of the ocean with the woman she loved, her shitty cat, and not having to truly die just yet. Let the rest of the world fight, she was ready for a damned vacation.

Dearest Clementine,

I did it! Dear heavenly stars, I did it! The bottle of blood is in my grasp, and I'm going to unlock the door now. The mountain fiend gave me the blood without me having to demand it, but I did have to give up a piece of myself. But we are all only a pile of broken pieces, are we not? My heart is beating faster and faster because I'll see you soon, I swear. This story is my heart to you.

Always Yours,
Dorin

Wrong is Possibly Right
1742

*I*n a remote land, hidden deep within snowy-white woods, lived a girl who was not really a girl at all. She was a winter creature who tore and ripped apart any human life that entered her territory. Not because she hated them, but because her home could *not* be found. She would protect it—always.

In those same snowy-white woods lived a boy who was not really a boy at all. He had long horns and pointy ears and when he went out of those woods to perform his macabre duty, he became a vicious beast and searched out naughty children who deserved what they got.

The girl hated the boy, but the boy never once hated the girl.

Marlena dangled from a thick branch by her knees, swinging back and forth, her long white hair swaying along with her. She let the dizziness consume her and only thought of happy things.

Until a sound came from up the icy path behind the cluster of trees. She swooped back up and rested easily on her haunches. Inhaling, she took a deep whiff of the air and stilled—*human*.

Why can't they stop being so curious? she thought, shifting forward to press her fingertips to the cold branch.

Her duty in the woods was to end the lives of anyone who entered her territory. It was to protect not only her, but those she loved. Those that were hidden deep below the surface and those that were out in the open.

A male human, a few years older than Marlena, entered the snow-covered clearing beneath her. As his boots plowed and crunched through the snowy ground, he didn't once look up at her. The human's thick black hair was tied back, and a tawny-colored cloak made from animal fur covered him fully. His eyes filled with wonder as he gazed around her home at the curving trees, the slivers of icicles, the icy flowers.

Nothing was supposed to grow here—her world was too cold. However, there were trees created from ice and leaves made from snow. As Marlena breathed in the crisp air and watched the human peer around her woods in fascination, she imagined him spreading word of this magical place throughout his village.

Marlena ran her tongue across her pointy teeth. She took a measured step across the branch, a low creaking coming from it as a crack erupted beneath her bare feet. The man's head jerked toward hers, but he didn't reach for his blade. They never did. He was possibly too entranced by her looks—which must have been strange to him—or perhaps he was a bit curious.

"What are you?" he asked, searching her face, the

two small horns on her forehead, and the fur she wore that didn't cover her arms or legs.

"You shouldn't have come here," Marlena said, her voice condescending. "I'm sorry, but humans cannot hold secrets well." With those words, she dove from the tree, the freezing air striking her face. Her feet struck the snow with a heavy thud. Right as the man's hand went to his hip for his weapon, his throat was slashed by her ivory blade, and his body slumped to the ground. Liquid from the man's torn neck turned the snow crimson.

As she lowered her head, the metallic scent hit her nostrils. She pressed two long fingers to her lips and let out a low whistle, loud enough for the creatures of the snowy woods to hear. From behind the pearlescent trees and buried beneath the snow, little round, naked creatures with loose, clear skin rose from their homes. Bones could be seen under their translucent selves, and their teeth clicked together as they came forward for the wondrous feast bestowed on them.

Fur cloak and clothing from the man was ripped away and his skin eaten, followed by muscle, then bones, until nothing was left of the intruder. Even the blood that had scattered across the snow had been lapped up.

Something touched Marlena's bare foot, and she looked down to one of the bald creatures nudging her leg. She knelt and petted the top of its head, the creature's pointy ears wiggling. "Thank you," she said.

To her left, another one pulled on the edge of her shirt. She turned around to see him holding up a kidney that she'd thought had already been consumed.

"No." She shooed the darling away. "Go on."

He shook his head, clicked his tongue, and held it up again. These small creatures of her woods meant everything to her, and Marlena would sacrifice for them over and over again.

She gripped his small hands between hers, the blood from the organ already cool between them both. "I can't."

After realizing that Marlena would not be taking his food as a gift, the creature nodded and waddled away.

Marlena's stomach stirred with hunger, but her food of choice was the snow leaves from the trees. She plucked several and listened to them crunch in between her teeth, before sliding down her tongue.

The taste was almost euphoric.

As she reached for another one, the loud sound of clinking bells echoed behind her. Without turning around to the new guest, she let out an annoyed and frustrated breath. He was back sooner than she'd thought he would be.

It only took seconds, but a large shadow now hovered above her. She barely glanced over her shoulder to see the snow creature behind her. His fur was whiter than falling flurries, his horns a lightly tinted blue. He looked as if he could be destined for what the humans called the heavens, but he was not—he was a murderous beast.

So am I, she thought. *So am I*. But she always justified her murders as being a must, or everyone and everything she loved would falter and die if they were discovered.

Without peering down, Marlena knew a fragile human child would lie in his arms. Steam came from his beastly snout as his warm breaths mingled with the cold air.

And his name was Krampus.

"You aren't supposed to be doing that," she snapped, meeting the blackness of his eyes. "It's only supposed to be one night a year, and murder does not qualify as the punishment you are supposed to give."

"The sins of the wicked are what keeps this place thriving, are they not?" Kram asked, his fangs protruding.

"So does the good." Marlena curled back her lips to show her sharpened teeth for him to see that she could be just as dangerous as him—if not more.

"The good may be the seeds of this place"—Kram said, cradling the small boy with hair the color of twilight—"but it is the wicked who are the rain and the sun that keep things alive."

"You always have an answer for everything, don't you?" Marlena seethed, taking a step away from him, and training her eyes on the necklace of bells around his throat.

"Go discuss it with the king and queen down below, then."

"I've tried…" Did he think she hadn't had conversations with them? *Without Krampus, your world would die,* they said. *Without Krampus, you would die.*

Marlena clenched her fists, then released them and held out her arms because there was nothing else she could say. "Give me the child." The boy was already dead and the only thing left to do was feed the land.

Kram's shoulders tensed and he pulled the still-form child closer to his chest. "I'll handle it."

Closing her eyes and grinding her teeth, Marlena turned around and led Kram down the uneven path to the largest ice tree in the woods. It was the heartbeat of this place, an eternal cure to everyone born there. Each gnarled branch was cloaked in snow and icy thorns. Lifting her hand, she knocked three times against the hard trunk.

In answer, roots erupted from the ground, shuffling forward and backward, their heavy groans piercing her pointed ears. Near the front of the tree, a space at its base opened, creating a shallow hole. Kram inched forward to a kneeling position and tucked the small boy inside.

With more groans and moans, the roots twitched and wiggled, caging the dead body of the boy. The sacrifice became completely covered and Marlena knew the boy was being consumed by the tree.

Fluffy snow fell from the sky at that moment, gathering on Marlena's lashes until she could hardly see.

After wiping most of the flakes away, her gaze met the blackened eyes of Kram, his body swaying back and forth.

"Did you drink too much of the human's wine?" Marlena knew he liked to indulge in the drink from the village at times.

"No, I..." Kram's eyes fluttered before his body collapsed and thumped into the snow. His fur shriveled away, leaving his form naked, besides for the bells around his neck. Two horns, like hers, sat on his forehead—matching pairs were at the sides of his wrists and ankles. His white hair cascaded just past his shoulders, and his pointed ears peeked out from in between the locks.

Marlena's eyebrows lowered as her eyes narrowed to the thinnest of slits. A small gasp escaped her throat when her gaze connected with three arrows protruding from his back.

"Kram!" she shouted, falling to the snow. Frantically, she reached out with her long fingers and tried shaking him awake.

Isn't this what I always wanted? she wondered. *For him to not exist?* Grasping his large arms, Marlena dragged him back as far as she could, which wasn't very far at all. She pressed her hands against his temples and twisted his head to the side so he wasn't suffocating in the snow.

As she yanked each arrow from his back, she didn't try to be nice or gentle. Kram didn't twitch or jerk, only stayed perfectly still. He should have been more careful, should not have let himself be seen, should not have been hunting small children who really didn't know right from wrong. Earlier, the man who had entered her territory was a person who knew the difference between those two things, even if he had wandered in by accident.

Kram's wounds didn't heal right away, and he lay still against the ground. Scrunching her nose, Marlena picked up one of the arrows and touched the pointed tip. She let out a shrill shriek and tossed the weapon down. *Iron. They know.*

Fear, deep and wretched, entered her heart. Someone from the village knew what Kram was, but did they know where he hailed from?

She dropped beside Kram and placed a hand against his cool cheek. It was the first time she had ever touched him. She always stood far from him, never wanting to get close to the child murderer. "Wake up!"

His eyelids flickered open, and specks of white glittered against the obsidian color of his eyes as if the night sky were buried there. Studying her for a brief moment, he then yanked his head away from her palm and scurried to sit up. Kram's naked form was pebbling over with gooseflesh.

"I think you should come inside." Marlena didn't really want him in her home, but she didn't want to anger the king or queen either if he died.

"I can go home."

She wished he would.

"No"—Marlena motioned him to follow her—"you are coming inside. We have much to talk about."

She didn't offer to help Kram to stand as he struggled to push himself up from the ground. After walking several paces away, past icy foliage and sharp bushes covered in ivory berries, they came to a stop in front of her cozy cottage. Her home rested just below the inside of the tree. The tree's snowy leaves and branches reached to the skies, and her image reflected in the sheen of ice frozen to the trunk. Producing a golden key from her hidden pocket, she unlocked the door at its base.

Marlena opened the secluded door and walked down the few steps to the open area. She crossed the room to her nest of twigs and dried leaves that came from outside her woods. Kram's heavy footsteps echoed behind her. Snatching the folded silk blanket from her bed, she tossed it to him. Kram struck the blanket with his hand as if she were giving him poison. It fell to the floor in a puddle of wrinkles.

She ignored his strange behavior. "You need to warm yourself while your body tries to heal from the iron."

Kram glanced toward the back of her home at the small lake. It glistened a pale-blue and twinkled with specks of white. Then his gaze peered at her golden objects hanging on the walls—cups, spoons, forks, plates. She liked the way it looked—Kram appeared not to. Before she yelled at him to pick up the blanket, he did so, and wrapped the soft blue silk around his large body as he sat on the ground beside her nest.

"How are your wounds?" Marlena asked, folding her arms over her chest.

He flicked his hand in the air as though he hadn't put his life or her woods at risk. "They're already gone."

"How did they know *what* you are?"

"Because one saw me." Kram kept his gaze focused on the wall of her collections, not meeting her angry stare.

"And you didn't *kill* this human?" Marlena spat, crouching down in front of him so he would have to look at her.

Kram sighed and turned his head to meet her icy stare, their faces only a whisper apart. "I only kill the ones I have to."

"We are going into the village tonight," she said, pointing at him and then herself, "and if you won't kill this human, then I will."

When he didn't respond and glanced away, she snatched his chin to make sure he didn't look away again. "What is it? Will you only murder children?"

"Let me show you something first," he whispered, his dark eyes hiding whatever he was truly thinking, "before you start your rampage."

"Fine." Marlena let go of his chin and walked away to gather the necessities that she would bring with her to stop the threat.

When the ice village turned dark, and the trees glistened under the pale moonlight, Marlena and Kram made their first move toward the village. She lit a piece of ice with blue fire, and even as they exited the woods, it stayed lit by the magic.

Kram had changed into what she called his demon form, cloaked in his thick white fur, and his blue horns appearing longer than ever before. Perhaps it was only her imagination about the horns.

The town's village grew near, with its rows of homes in neat lines, going on and on. Reclining his head back, Kram wrinkled his snout and took a long sniff of the air. He wiggled a finger for her to follow closely behind him. She pressed her hand against the blue fire and snuffed it out.

Keeping as silent as they could under the night sky, they padded through tall weeds and entered a village. After passing several stone cottages covered in ivy, and warm light in the windows, Kram halted in front of a small hut with a cracked window. Marlena stopped behind him, watching him place a furred finger to his snout. He unlocked a bell from around his neck and cracked it open, bits of dust falling into his palm. With a quick thrust, he tossed the dust into the air on her.

The strange dust glittered bright white for a moment before fluttering out. "Will this keep me quiet?" she whispered.

"If only it would keep you quiet to me," he said, reaching for the door.

Her anger only intensified but she didn't say anything else.

With slow movements, Kram opened the door and stepped inside, Marlena trailing behind him. The house remained silent as they peered around, the occupants presumably asleep throughout the hut. Decapitated animal heads lined the sitting room walls, along with wooden furniture draped in furs. Marlena shuddered to herself because she knew if this human ever found out about her woods, there would be the snowy creatures' heads on the walls, too. Two candles flickered in the hallway, as though hinting at the human's life coming to an end in moments.

Up ahead, down a narrow hallway, rested three doors, two completely shut and the other cracked open. Kram pushed open the cracked one and stepped inside, the bells around his neck jangling.

Something in the bed stirred and made a light,

muffled sound. Kram held out his furred arm to prevent Marlena from moving forward. The noise receded into light breathing, and Marlena slid out the knife of ice from her belt. She edged to the sleeping human until her knees pressed to the bed, to where she saw … a child. Long, golden locks framed her innocent face.

Marlena's head twisted to Kram, her lip curling and her hand gripping the ice so tightly it started to crack. "This is the person who shot you?"

"No…" He didn't look at the child, only at her. "But she's the one calling to me."

"You brought me here so I can watch you kill a child? You truly are demonic." If he wasn't so greatly beloved by the royalty underground, she would have stopped his heart right then and there.

"No, Marlena." He reached out to press a hand to what she thought was her shoulder, but the fury on her face must have made him think better about it because he brought it back down to his side. "The girl's father is the one who shot me, but I'm going to show you something. And you alone. You have to understand why I do what I do. Do you trust me?"

Before she could give him her answer, which would have been *never*, Kram's claws extended, and he stabbed one directly into the child's heart. The young girl's eyes flew open and a choked sound escaped her throat, gasping for air. Marlena straightened her spine as she watched the human child fade back into what appeared to be sleep, but was not.

With her brows furrowed and lips curled in disgust, Marlena watched as Kram peeled open the girl's mouth and drew out the tongue. Using his long claw, he cut open his hand and let his blood spill against the tongue. To Marlena's horror, he handed it to her.

"Eat it."

Once more, he shook his hand at her when she didn't retrieve it.

"What?" she screeched, no longer disgusted but angry, and possibly a bit fearful. "No."

"If you want to know my secrets," he murmured, almost melancholic, "then eat it."

There was something in his expression that made her eyes narrow a bit less, her jaw slacken a bit more. She still didn't trust him. But if there were secrets hidden behind those large black eyes of his, then she wanted to know them.

She swiped the small piece of human life from his furry hand and quickly placed it into her mouth. At first she tasted a certain sweetness from his blood, but something foul lay beneath as her teeth chewed. She could only imagine it to be rot, and it became worse, so much so that she could barely breathe. Her hands flew to her throat. "You tricked me!"

Kram didn't reach out to help her. Instead, his demonic eyes only studied her.

Dropping to her knees, Marlena spat out what she could of the tongue, but it was too late.

Visions flashed through her head.

The girl in bed, Livy, is no longer dead, but instead, grows into a woman of around eighteen seasons. Livy has become more horrid with the passing of each year, stealing from others while letting innocents take fault. A friend of hers has fallen in love with a boy who Livy is infatuated with. She secretly murders the girl and lets the boy find comfort in her.

On a hunt, Livy finds her way to the snowy woods, where she encounters Marlena. An arrow from Livy's bow strikes Marlena's chest and another her skull. Marlena falls from her perched position in a tree, her body and neck at awkward angles in the snow below.

The images vanished, pulling Marlena back to the present.

She rubbed a hand repeatedly against her own tongue to rid herself of the bitterness and the image. But the foul taste still lingered.

When Marlena's gaze connected with Kram's, he said, "The human who shot me is down the hall." He didn't say anything else as he lifted the girl, Livy, into his arms. Marlena didn't stop him.

She remembered there was still a man she needed to find, so she padded down the hallway, and flung open the door. A man beneath a thick blanket lightly snored, but there was no one else in sight.

Despite trying to brush off the thoughts of the terrible girl, she couldn't. To distract herself, Marlena crept closer, took out her knife, and pushed it into the heart of the man who could bring harm to her woods. The man's horrible eyelids opened. She then pushed her blade into each eye so even in death he wouldn't be able to see her or her snowy home.

Taking a deep breath, she pulled back and held the bloody knife to her chest. For now, everyone would be safe.

In the doorway, Kram nodded, telling her that it was time to leave. The dead child rested in his arms, and Marlena didn't say a word.

The entire short journey back home, they both remained silent. Marlena waited and waited for Kram to say something, but he didn't. She couldn't hold anything in any longer.

"That ... that wasn't a normal human child," she said softly.

"No ... no, it wasn't." He confirmed the suspicions that she had gone over and over as they walked in the night.

"You murder them because you know they are going to grow to be monstrous."

"Yes."

The thought of what lay beyond the image of where she had died frightened Marlena to her very core. *What would have happened to everyone else in my woods?*

"Of course," Kram started, "there are too many in the world to stop, and at times they hide it too well. I can only find the ones who call to me."

She nodded, yet still wondered so many things, had so many questions. But then the great tree came into their line of sight, its thorny branches shivering in hunger. Even though the thing in Kram's arms was still a human child, Marlena didn't think of it as one any longer.

Kram was not the demon, the children he brought back were. Livy was a devious little creature who would grow up to make Marlena's world suffer.

She knocked on the trunk three times. The tree creaked and groaned, causing the land to tremble under her feet as it lifted its large roots to make the hole appear. Kram placed the fragile body inside, and they watched the hole close back up, taking the child in to devour. With his head lowered, Kram turned to walk away. Marlena now knew he didn't take pleasure in doing these deeds. Something inside her chipped away and her heart sped up as she watched him.

"Come inside," Marlena said. "I need to get cleaned up."

For a moment she didn't think he would follow her as she made her way toward her home, but then she heard the thumping of his footsteps from behind.

After Kram entered her home, he shed his furred-body until he stood before her in his naked form.

"You really should have more manners." Marlena's tone was serious, but a smidge of playfulness came with it. She tossed him the same silk blanket he had used earlier, and he caught it this time instead of fighting it as if it were going to bite him. He wrapped it around himself as she motioned him toward the bathing area.

She removed her fur clothing and pushed her legs into the cool, glistening water before fully submerging her body. Kram sat with the blanket over his shoulders but didn't touch her water as she washed off the blood from her face and hands, along with the grime.

Marlena squeezed out her hair and stepped out from the water. Kram lifted his arm, holding out the blanket. She stared at the open area beside him while biting her lip, contemplating whether to get dressed first. But she chose to sit next to him and let herself dry a bit. He covered them both with the blanket, and his skin felt less cool against hers, to the point where it was possibly a warm feeling. True warmth was something she could never feel, but a hint of it seemed to be there—between the two of them.

She thought about the image one more time that he'd shown her, and focused on how the vision had included *her*. There had to be more to it. "You don't only kill them for the tree and their sins, do you?"

He released a shaky breath, holding her tighter. "No." It was hard for Marlena to get a full answer from Kram, and she would have to fight it out of him.

"You scout out the ones who will destroy the woods?"

He shook his head, and his body shivered as she scooted even closer to his naked form.

"But I saw it." Her long fingers tapped against her leg. "The human girl came into the woods and killed me."

"That's right."

"And then…"

"No and then." He paused and stared up at the ceiling. "I go after the ones who call to me first, who I know will destroy you."

Marlena's lips parted and for the first time in her life, she was at a loss for words. "But you don't even like me."

"I've always liked you, Marlena." He smiled, almost sadly. "You're the one who thinks I'm dirt beneath the snow."

"I do think that." She had always thought that.

He nodded and let out a heavy breath as if he had said too much. "Do you still?"

"No, not as much." Her tone was gentle and she looked at him, for the first time truly *looked* at him. His blue horns were shorter in this form, his lips pursed together, his large pointed ears tipped out from his long white hair. They were all only features, but his dark eyes that she always believed to be ones of a demon, didn't feel that way any longer. The glassiness of the color reflected everything she needed to see.

"Perhaps," Kram asked, "one day you might like me?"

Before she fully stood, Marlena knelt in front of him, placing her hands on his shoulders. She pressed her lips against his and held them there for a long moment, feeling the warmth that she didn't know was possible.

"Perhaps," Marlena said and pulled away. She walked to her nest with a smile on her face and a vengeance in her heart to not only protect the woods, but also to protect Kram.

Marlena would wait for him to come to her in her nest, where she would look forward to discovering what new and magical warmth they could create together next.

Dearest Clementine,

I'm piecing this book together for you now. I didn't know if I would be able to give it to you or not. Truly, I did not. But I found you, and it wasn't me who saved you, was it? You had already done it alone—defeated Bogdi. You reached within yourself and produced the fiery flames that had always been there, burning his demonic soul to ash. All I had to do was unlock the door to let you out. Last night was one of the most profound moments of my life, not because of your kisses and touches but because in the end, we figured out a way to beat Bogdi while being apart. Your heart may be a bit darkened now, and I may be missing a part of myself, but our love is stronger than ever. These stories were all for you, and one day, I hope to read the tale that you plan to write me.

Always Yours,
Dorin

Bonus Short Story

Dearest Dorin: A Romantic Ghostly Tale

For those who believe that love always wins

♥

Dearest Dorin,

You once penned me the most miraculous stories, and in return you had hoped I would spin you a tale. The time has finally come. Now, I don't have as many as you had, but I do have one. My time away with that awful demon, Bogdi, had quite the effect on me, but through it all, I held on to my love for you, as you have for me. As you know, I defeated him by reaching into my fiendish self, where I gathered the flames to burn him to ash, all while ripping out his heart. It's quite funny how that almost goes with some of your stories, my love. Anyway, this is for you, and you alone.

Love Always,
Clementine

Ghosts of the Past
1972

Step one: enter the home. Step two: find the signs. Step three: remove the ghosts.

Cate shouldered her backpack and read over the letter one more time. In her hand was the payment check, her name written in cursive across the front of the envelope.

Dear Cate,

I hear you're the best at what you do. My home is filled with a presence that I yearn to be rid of. I hope you decide to come. The rest of the payment at the end will be great.

Deacon Jax
515 Bayridge Rd

Deacon Jax… She hadn't heard of the name before. But she recognized the street name, just farther up the road. Cate tapped the yellowing letter against her thigh. This could be just what she needed, and if she rid Mr. Jax's house of the ghosts, maybe it was possible to find higher-paying jobs like this one. Her excitement grew at the thought, the money, the prospects.

But she didn't understand why he'd just left a letter

when the street wasn't that far away. The back of her head throbbed and she pressed her hand against it—she was thinking too much and too positively at the moment.

"Focus, Cate. You haven't even gotten through this job yet."

Her head pulsed again. *Stupid headache*. She hoped it would dull soon.

The money was important here, and if she didn't take this job, she would need to find a real one. She couldn't go back to waitressing. Her mind preferred to try and solve the unknown with her ghost-hunting partner... He wasn't with her anymore, be it friend, ghost-hunting partner, lover. He was gone, and no longer by her side. She needed to stop loving him, because he hadn't loved her enough to stay. There was no point for her to even think about his name when she was already forgetting what his face even looked like.

She folded the letter and slipped it into her pocket, then lifted her briefcase filled with all the things she'd need for the weeklong event. Tape recorder, ghost-detecting rods, herbs, Ouija board. Tapping her chin, Cate tried to recollect if she was missing something. As soon as she arrived, she was sure something would come up.

Blowing out a breath, she adjusted her backpack and walked the two miles up the road to where her destination was. Her car was indisposed, but she preferred going on foot when possible. Cate had skipped breakfast because she hadn't felt hungry, not when there was a ghost job to be done. Several cars sped past her, driving way too fast, kicking up gravel and other bits, giving her a dust bath that she hadn't asked for.

"Thanks, fuckers!" she yelled, even though the drivers had their windows rolled up and probably couldn't hear her anyway.

A black metal sign with the word *Bayridge Rd* pointed left and she turned down the road that was filled with overgrown grass and no sidewalks. Cate had passed this way but had never found the need to go down most of the streets in this part of town. In fact, the farther she got, the more houses became sparse, until there were none.

Am I on the right street?

Oak trees with cascading moss blocked most of the view until, up ahead, the sun shone down at the peak of a grassy hill. Cate stopped in her tracks where her gaze met a long metal fence with sharp points that looked like spears. The rusted fence enclosed the entire property, elm trees and a luscious lawn visible through it. And there, in the distance, stood an imposing mansion looming over it all. She shuffled toward the fence, brushing her fingertips against the cool steel, and peered in between the narrow posts. Taking in the home's massive form, Cate's gaze fell to a tiny rectangular window with iron bars that no one could possibly fit through, leading somewhere into the unknown.

At the back of the house, the edge of the yard dropped off into the bay where she knew there would be enormous, cutting rocks below. She closed her eyes and listened to the sounds of the water pressing its body to the earth in slow strikes. If she felt like dying, which she didn't, she could easily walk the path and plunge straight down to her end. That wasn't an option for her. But when she did one day pass, she hoped it would be through falling.... Falling as though flying, until the collision with earth shattered her body. Her head pulsed and she shook off the dark thought.

Cate opened the already unlocked gate and padded inside, the world around her chilly as the morning wind blew. She wished she'd packed a sweater. That was the item she'd forgotten.

The mansion appeared lonely, as though it needed an acquaintance. She inexplicably felt like she was in a horror story of her own, but it was always like that since she hunted ghosts for a living. She had a duty to uncover what was disturbing her clients, and within a week tops, she would set this man free, too.

Swiftly, Cate moved across the grass, the moist blades tickling her bare ankles. A light fog spilled from the water in swaying motions, but not strong enough to pull forward and embrace the mansion, or her.

Cate's heart beat at the readiness, wondering what sort of spirit she'd find. Up close, the mansion's roof looked in need of repair with several missing shingles. Window after window lined the front, each one covered in grime. Thick green vines, with small leaves, latched on to most of the outside, and the parts that were unveiled showed chipped paint in all the right places, making the home appear even eerier than it should've been.

When the place had first been built, she bet it had been quite the sight. It still was now, possibly even more so, only in a different way.

Cate noticed there had been a garden at one point, but all the rosebushes were now dead, not a single green leaf in sight. She imagined Mr. Jax to be an elderly man, living a reclusive life.

As Cate stepped on the modest porch, she peered at the ghost statue on the ground, then up at the tall metal door. The round knocker had a face on it of a werewolf, like one from an old monster film. Cate grinned as she reached for it, knocking on the massive door twice. Before she could knock a third time, the door flung open, tearing the knocker from her grip, and she stepped back.

"Cate? Is that you?" The voice sounded full of desperation, the speaker out of breath, as if he'd run to answer the door. Cate prepared herself to calm an overly reactive client. She should be used to this by now—most of them could be almost irrational at times.

After adjusting her briefcase, she swung her head back up to meet the eyes of the man who could quite possibly be the kind who would jump at every noise, scaring himself to the point of insanity by imagining ghosts at every creak, and hearing spirits with every roar of the wind.

Instead, the man who answered the door was not elderly as she'd thought. He was young, in his early twenties at the most, like herself. And attractive ... like a young Vincent Price.

Cate's breath caught and she gulped as she met the man's bright blue eyes. He was slender, elegant even, his features pretty, rather than ruggedly handsome. Appearing nervous, he ran a hand through short dark hair, and lowered thick lashes. Cate couldn't help but notice how smooth the skin of his long fingers looked. How soft his lips seemed...

What the ever-loving hell was wrong with her? Was she going to stand there and gawk at a handsome client's every feature?

No. She loved her partner still. Even if he'd left her, even if he didn't feel the same.

And yet... Something about this man drew Cate's attention.

No! she told herself again. She needed to pull herself together and stop acting like she'd never seen a boy—man—before. This man was a client. A client who was watching her—watching him—and waiting for her to do her damn job.

"Mr. Jax?" Cate asked, straightening, and avoided looking at his face.

"Yes, that's me," he said with a smile that she noticed when her eyes shifted back in his direction. "But call me Deacon."

"All right, Deacon." Cate smiled in return, then noticed his fingers were still twitching at his sides as she reached to open her briefcase. "Do you need something to calm your nerves?"

"Like drugs?" His forehead and nose wrinkled in confusion.

"No! Like tea!" She laughed. "I have some packets with me, if you needed some."

"Oh," Deacon started, clearing his throat. "I wouldn't have taken drugs if you'd offered them, but it just sounded like that's what you were referring to. But I don't need tea, either. Go ahead and come inside." He motioned her in.

"Um, all right." She gave him the barest of smiles, finding his awkwardness rather cute as she stepped inside his home. *Time to get to work, Cate.*

The edginess was something she was used to anyway. When Cate was a child, she'd been frightened at first when she'd discovered she could see things from the beyond. But when she found out that she could use her ability to help others, it had changed things for her.

Around her, the house seemed to sigh, and she tried to catch a flicker of any movement that shouldn't be there. She wasn't sure what she would have to do here just yet. But it always felt good to help others pass to the lighter side, or push them back into their dark place where they belonged.

"I can feel a presence," Cate said, setting down her briefcase and fishing out her notebook and a pen from her backpack. She scribbled a few sentences down about her thoughts so far. "How long has this been going on?"

Deacon rubbed both hands slowly down his face from forehead to chin, his pinkies remaining on his lower lip while the others stayed planted on his cheeks. "Too long."

"And you're just now seeking help?" Her eyes widened. He'd been here all this time, living with ghosts, and doing nothing about it?

Deacon nodded, his expression neutral. "Yes."

"And you've just been … avoiding the issue?"

"I guess, but things have been progressing, getting worse, tormenting me. She haunts me at times and won't always listen."

This one was a real Edgar Allan Poe, it seemed. "So it's a she?"

"There's more than one, but you can tell me, since you're the expert."

"Well, I can start the first day by leaving the tape recorders out and come back in the morning to see what I find." Some people preferred that, even though she'd brought all her things with her. He hadn't been very specific in the letter, now that she thought about it.

"No!" he said hurriedly, mussing his hair in all directions. "I mean, you can stay here. As you could probably tell from the outside, there are plenty of available rooms."

She thought back to the basement with the iron bars attached to the bottom of the house, and most people would decide to hightail it right then. But she wasn't most. She knew how to kick someone's ass from her Taekwondo days and could get him on his back in under a second if need be.

There was always the hidden chance that this man could be a regular Jack the Ripper knockoff, and if that were so, then this would make it all the more of a challenge. She yearned for the whispering dare, and if she could solve a serial crime instead, that would put her name straight into the paper.

Yet something about Deacon's dark blue eyes, the emotion lingering there, told her he wasn't a murderer. He just had other spiritual problems to deal with.

A swishing stirred from behind Cate, catching her off guard. A cold gust of wind cascaded down the spiral staircase, spinning around her, and rumpling her hair. She knew then that even if he was a serial killer, there was also clearly a presence here, and not a good one at that. The ghosts who wanted to play nice usually roamed the halls moaning, or rocked in their chairs, or tried to start conversations with walls, sometimes with her. They didn't hurl gusts of winds or make houses speak. This was something purely evil she had on her hands.

Carefully, Cate eyed the room to make sure no weapons could be launched her way—the coast was clear. Only paintings of wilting flowers hung on the walls. A red velvet sofa sat in the middle of the room, and to its side rested a black chaise in front of an oval coffee table. Farther down was a fireplace and a stack of chopped wood.

Her gaze swept back to Deacon, who was politely studying her, waiting for her answer.

"I'll stay the night here, but my room must have a lock on it."

"That can easily be arranged. All the bedrooms are on the second floor, and they all have a lock on them." He waved her forward and took the briefcase from her hand—his fingers lightly touched hers—like a proper gentleman. Even though she'd have a lock on her door, it wouldn't really matter since he'd have a key. But it would still give her enough time to grab her pistol if she heard the sound of someone, or something, unlocking her door.

Cate followed his slender frame up the winding staircase, covered in thick and fluffy red carpet. She skimmed her palm up the wooden rail as she peered at more paintings of what looked to be from

Shakespearean plays.

At the top of the stairs, Deacon led her down a hall lined with a long, ornate gold and silver rug. Bronze molded hands decorated the walls, and she found them fascinating, as each one held its fingers in different positions.

"These are neat."

"They are. I didn't pick them out, though." Deacon came to a stop in front of a cream-colored door and tapped the wood with his pointer finger. "This is your room. Mine is directly across from it ... if you should need me." His gaze molded to hers, and she didn't want to look away, but she needed to focus on the job at hand.

"I'm already taken," Cate lied, or sort of. She still couldn't help but love someone she should be trying to forget.

"I didn't mean it like that." Deacon held up his hands, his face twisted in a cringe. "What I meant to say was only if something stirs in there. My room seems to be the safest."

She let out a nervous laugh and rubbed her temple when the ache triggered again from her sudden movement. "Oh, now I feel stupid. I'm so sorry."

"Don't be." His fingers twitched and tapped his leg as he scanned everything across the hall, except for her face. "But maybe you should stay with me, just in case."

She almost reached out to place a hand on Deacon's shoulder to stop his nervous twitching. But something told her touching him might not be the best idea, especially with how she reacted when he'd answered the front door. "No, I'll be fine. If I feel like I need the offer, then I'll come to you." She then cringed as well because she wouldn't be coming to *him*, only to his room if need be.

They both stood there, not saying anything else, as her heart beat furiously within her chest. "I guess I'll start unpacking my things, so I can begin placing tape recorders around the house." She grabbed the rose-shaped knob and opened the door, stepping inside.

Cate had expected the room to be full of dust based on what she'd seen on the outside of the house, but it wasn't. In fact, it looked as though it had just been cleaned. A knitted blanket was strewn across the mattress, and spiral designs were carved into the wooden headboard. An oval mirror connected to an antique desk rested in the corner, while a clothing wardrobe stood on the opposite side.

Black candles lined the walls in silver cradles, along with paintings of *Phantom of the Opera* and *Nosferatu*. Everything was wonderfully gothic, as though she'd just arrived at the home of the Addams Family. It gave the circumstances the perfect, yet familiar touch.

"Lunch will be ready shortly." Deacon didn't turn away as he paused, waiting to see what she would say.

"Who's cooking? Do you have any staff here?" She didn't see how he'd be able to take care of this mansion after seeing the inside. The cleaning alone would be a full-time thing, but he'd have enough money to do that based on the half payment she'd received from him. Did he even have a real job?

"I'll be doing it, and no, only me." He bit his lower

lip. "Other than the ghosts, that is."

It hit her a moment too late that he was attempting a joke. She cracked a smile, just as she remembered not eating anything for breakfast. "All right, let me know when lunch is ready and I'll be there. I'm not one to pass up a meal, but I'm still going to start getting things set up, and later this evening we can use the Ouija for a bit."

"Aren't Ouijas supposed to, you know, make things worse?" He cocked his head as the sides of his lips lifted. "You make it sound like a bit of a game."

"I do like games. Here's a secret that I'll only let you in on." She paused, finding herself smiling, too. "For me that's not possible, because I'm the best."

Deacon rubbed his chin. "So confident."

She arched a brow and pressed a hand on her hip. "Of course, isn't that why you wrote to me?"

"One of the reasons." He shrugged, then spun on his heel and walked away.

She poked her head out the door to watch him descend the staircase. Deacon didn't once look back over his shoulder. He had nice shoulders, even though what he'd said had been odd. She shook her head at the thought.

As soon as she knew he'd completely vanished, Cate shut the door and locked it. If she heard a click, she'd grab her gun and be ready. But something in her gut told her she wouldn't need it. However, if guns could only be used on ghosts, then her weapon would get the job done a lot quicker.

Cate sank to the floor and pressed her back to the footboard of the bed. With anxious fingers strumming the air, she unlocked her briefcase and opened it, then drew out the six tape recorders and the Ouija board.

She padded her way across the room to the desk and set the first recorder there in front of the mirror before pressing play.

In a few moments, she'd find spots throughout the house to place the other ones, to see if any of the areas would pick up different sounds. Sometimes all, or a few of them, found hidden noises—other times, none of them did. There was always a mystery when playing Marco Polo with spirits.

Cate slid in earplugs to block out sounds as she rummaged through the briefcase under a stack of papers, until she found two dowsing rods. Each one was a straight line that formed an "L" shape. Slowly, she lifted the rods and held them out in front of her as she tiptoed across the room. The earplugs muffled any real noises, yet helped to increase the sounds of any unwanted guests.

Before her very eyes, the rods lost their parallel position and curved toward each other. A light tapping softly thrummed against the walls, like the pads of fingers rhythmically moving. *There is absolutely a presence here.*

Heart accelerating at what she might possibly uncover, Cate opened the door and headed out of the room. She cradled the recorders and rods in one arm while running her hand against the wall with the other. Each of the bronze hands on the wall wiggled their fingertips, a sigh escaping as the presence left, floating in the direction to the end of the hall. The hands halted their movement, but Cate followed where the sound had drifted, toward a cracked door. Heart hammering, she took long strides down the path until she reached the door. She drew the entrance wider and slowly went up the creaking wooden steps, only to find an attic filled with cardboard boxes.

Tilting her head, she took out the plugs and listened closely for any rumblings or whispers. None. Too late. With a sigh, Cate set down a tape recorder and wandered back down the stairs and out into the hall, checking for any more movements. While surveying the area, she placed another recorder outside one of the rooms.

As she passed by Deacon's door, her interest piqued. She started to turn and walk away, then she spun back around and reached for his doorknob, knowing good and well she should ask him first. But Cate did what she wanted at times, and lucky for her, the door was unlocked anyway. Besides, it would be nice to know more about the man she was spending the night with. She instead could've always asked him more about himself, but this was easier, more raw.

Thankfully, the door didn't echo a single creak when she slipped inside. As her eyes adjusted to the little light spilling in through the window, she found the room to be interesting with red and black striped walls. It appeared Deacon might be a collector. Also, possibly vain? An antique oval mirror hung on each wall. A desk matched the one from her room, except an old-fashioned typewriter sat on his. Next to the typewriter rested empty photograph frames, a stack of yellowed paper, and a collection of pens. It was all organized, with no speck of dust in sight.

Her attention fell on the row of drawers and she reached forward to pull one open when the door behind her poured in more light. She steeled her spine and glanced over her shoulder.

Deacon stilled. "What are you doing in here?"

Cate gripped the tape recorder and casually put it on the desk. "Spreading these everywhere." She brushed past him, as if it was no big deal, like she hadn't just become a spy in his house. "There's another in the hall, the attic, and in my room. I'm going to take these last two downstairs."

"Next time"—he blew out a breath, not appearing too agitated—"don't just go in my room, not unless I'm there."

"I thought you said your room is the safest part in the house," Cate pointed out. "But I understand. I'm sorry, and I should've asked first."

"No, it's fine, it's just... I can't talk about it right now." His Adam's apple bobbed as he took a step back.

Something in his eyes took on a mournful hue that made her want to hurry and change the subject. "How about showing me the basement?"

"You don't have to go down there."

"No, I think I should. Since you're paying me, I need to make sure I check each level of the house. Show me the way." A thought crossed Cate's mind—she needed to confirm that there were indeed no dead bodies in the house, only ghosts. There was always the possibility of them being hidden in the walls, though. She'd never uncovered anything like that, or she could start charging more if she had.

As she carefully descended the stairs, Deacon's

hand touched her lower back. Cate couldn't help but find it nice as she glanced at him, but he wasn't staring at her. It was as if he was doing it out of habit. He'd been different about his room, same as he was now. Did he have someone he missed, the way she did? Cate pressed away from the almost-comfortable touch, his hand leaving her, and she missed it.

Once Deacon opened the door to the basement, he flicked on the light. A chilly wind swept past them, causing her heart to flutter.

"You may have noticed a lot of wind," he said.

"And the bronze hands moving in the hall."

"The presence here seems to have no teeth until the day grows later."

That's how it was a lot of the time—darkness tended to be attached to night.

Quietly, Cate followed Deacon down the rickety steps, her gaze peering across the room. She'd expected the basement to be much larger than it was. Her shoulders hunched a little in disappointment, not because there weren't dead bodies, but because it was empty. The only thing inside, besides four bricked walls, was the glass window with the dark iron bars.

"I had planned to turn this into a film room with a projector and record player, but just never got around to it," Deacon said with a sad smile as he stared first at the window, then back at Cate.

"That would be a fun idea." It was something she'd be interested in having, too.

Stepping forward, she put a recorder on the bare floor and held up the dowsing rods while she walked around the room. As with the other levels, the rods slowly maneuvered toward each other.

"Not to interrupt you, but lunch has been ready," Deacon said. "It might be a little cold now."

"That's fine. I'm used to eating things cold. I get so busy and distracted at times after making something for me and my boyfriend, that he's already finished with his when I finally settle down to eat mine. But I must say, it tastes better that way." She should've said ex-boyfriend, but she didn't correct it, even though a part of her wanted to.

"I'm one who eats fast, but I'll deal with the cold if I have to." He chuckled and the sound tickled her ears in an almost delicious way.

"It seems most people do prefer things warm."

As they left the basement in comfortable silence, Cate held the rods up when they entered the main room. One of the metal bars spun in a slow circle. This house was full of *something*—every single space held a presence. She was almost gleeful about the increasing challenge. Before the week was up, she swore to herself that Deacon's home would be picked clean of the lingering dead.

Deacon moved in front of the fireplace and tossed in a log before starting a fire. He took a blanket from the sofa and sprawled it across the floor in front of the flames, in a sort of picnic style.

Her eyebrows flew up. "What is this?"

"Oh, you mentioned using the Ouija board later, and I thought this would be a good place to put it."

"Ouija board and a picnic?"

"No, that's not how I meant this to look." He winced. "Sorry, I can bring it all to the table first."

Cate waved him off. "This is fine." The thought of a picnic with a Ouija board sounded interesting, and she should've thought of this before on her ghost hunts. She ventured back up the stairs and collected the Ouija, along with the planchette.

A noise erupted, like glass breaking. She whirled around, expecting to see broken fragments across the floor. But the mirror was still whole.

Clutching the back of her head where it throbbed for a moment, she headed back downstairs with her heart pounding a little quicker. Once in the main room, she found food already on the floor. Two bowls of soup and two plates of vegetables appeared to already be cooled off, along with a loaf of bread that was absent of heat.

"Thank you," Cate said as she took a seat across from Deacon who was already digging into his bowl. She still wasn't hungry, too concerned with needing to work, but she would force herself to eat anyway.

"You're welcome."

She lifted a spoonful to her mouth, moaning at the coolness of it as it slid down her throat, even though the food was flavorless. Deacon watched her with a dark brow raised as he ate another bite.

After she finished eating, she rubbed her hands together in front of the fire. "This Ouija tends to work best for me after dusk, so, for now, I'll do more searching throughout the house."

"Oh." He looked as though he wanted to come.

"If you'd like to join in, you can. I'm used to most clients not wanting anything to do with this." The edges of her lips curved up. "But if you dare to come…"

"I think I'll push myself to be up to this challenge." He grinned. "Why don't you show me everything you do? Explain to me what the rods are for, and why the tape recorders?"

"Really? You're not afraid to learn?" She folded her arms across her chest and grinned back.

"Nah, not with you here. It might be a good idea in case the hauntings ever reoccur, then I wouldn't have to call you out again."

"That might break my bank then."

"Who am I kidding? I'm too much of a wuss to do it on my own." Deacon chuckled that beautiful laugh like he had earlier.

"All right, well, let's start with these." Cate held up the dowsing rods and explained to Deacon how a simple thing could detect possible energy. He asked a lot of questions, surprising her.

They spent the rest of the afternoon going through each room of the house, not finding anything beyond what they'd already discovered. She couldn't help but like having someone at her side again, even if it would only be for a little while.

The sun was already setting. Cate walked beside Deacon down the stairs to the sitting room. He threw another log into the dying fire before going into the kitchen to make dinner.

When he came back, he placed two plates with sandwiches and chips on the blanket. She took a bite and pressed her fingertips on the planchette. "Ready?"

"I suppose." He rested his fingers close to hers but not enough to where they were touching. Did she want them to touch? *Yes.* She shoved the thought back.

"Hello?" Cate asked before she thought more about what his finger next to hers would feel like. "Is anyone there?"

Silence answered.

"I want to know why this house is being haunted."

The planchette moved to the left, then started to slowly spin. She took in a deep breath of air as the triangular piece spelled out a word. *HERE*

"Now, tell me why you're here."

She whispered the letters aloud as the planchette pointed to each one before stilling. *TO REMEMBER*

"Did you die here?"

YES

"Did you lose someone?"

YES

"Do you want revenge?"

The planchette spun faster and faster, the speed increasing as it went to each letter, as if by magnetic force.

I NEED HER

"Who?"

CATE

She released the planchette, her breaths uneven, nerves on edge.

Deacon's chest rose heavily, and he sat back. "What's going on?"

"It's one of those kinds of ghosts. A spirit who wants to have fun and will give the answers it wants instead of real ones. Maybe even cause a little fright."

He blinked. "Well, it worked."

"I think I should wait down here a while and see

what happens. You don't have to stay. Go get some rest." If he was getting anxious now, his room would do him good since it was the safest.

"No, I'll stay with you." He looked around the room, fingers twitching, as though something would creep out at that moment. "Just in case."

"Your choice." Even though she didn't mind working alone, she was relieved he wanted to remain there, so she wouldn't have to compare it to what it was like when working with a partner.

Cate inspected the Ouija while Deacon took two pillows from the sofa.

"Do you have an extra blanket?" she asked.

He grabbed another from the sofa and sprawled it out on top of the other blanket. "I can go take one from the bed if you need more."

"No, it's all right." She wouldn't be sleeping anyway.

The night had fallen and she stayed up with her legs crossed as noises creaked and moaned within the quiet of the house. A sound came from the ceiling, like leaking, but when she glanced up, nothing was dripping. Then around her, from her periphery, she caught wind of movement. Something wet was rising from the floor—bright red in color—blood. She stood still as a cascade of scarlet swirled around them, blanketing her and Deacon inside what looked to be a bloody funnel.

He scooted closer and pressed his hand to her back. "It won't hurt you."

But how could he be sure? Cate had never seen anything like this before—she stuck her hand out and the blood passed right through. She watched with wide eyes as everything drifted away toward the front door, spiraling, and vanishing. Pushing herself up from the floor, she scrambled for the door, only to find it locked, even when she unbolted it. Cursing at the door, she tried to yank it several more times.

"Does it do this every night?" Cate looked over her shoulder at Deacon who hadn't moved. "Lock you in?"

He nodded. "It's not going to let you leave until morning. The phones haven't worked in a while, either. That's why I left you the letter."

"You could've warned me before." Frowning, Cate released her hold on the door and walked back toward Deacon.

"I thought you were the professional. You know that ghosts do mysterious things."

"That's not telling everything!"

"Sorry?"

"You're not sorry, are you?"

"Well, no." He bit his lip. "Are you worried about your boyfriend?"

He wasn't with her. He'd left her behind, no longer her partner either. His face wasn't even as clear as the one of the man right before her. She decided to tell Deacon because she was tired of shouldering this burden. "I'm not really with him anymore."

"Oh." His eyebrows lifted. "How long has it been?"

"I don't know. A while." She shrugged as if it was nothing, but it wasn't nothing. It made her head hurt.

"But you still love him."

"I do."

"Can you imagine me as him, for the night?"

"What?" She almost laughed, but she was too shocked to do that at his sudden forwardness.

"I haven't ... in a while."

"You want me to sleep with you?" she screeched. "Like a prostitute for money?"

He held up his hands. "No! I mean, maybe... But not for money."

"That's a no." But a part of her was curious to find out what his lips would feel like against hers—she couldn't deny he was one of the most beautiful men she'd ever seen. Cate pushed that thought away.

"All right, then." He nervously moved a chip around on his plate. "Um, let's go back to what we were doing."

Back in the funnel of blood or back to the Ouija board? "So you want us to spend the night down here, in your ghost mansion, as if you didn't just ask me to have sex with you?" She wasn't going to just let what he'd said go.

"Yes."

"All right..."

"I won't try anything." He paused, not meeting her eyes. "Unless you want to, that is..."

Cate was locked in this house with this man who was attractive and nice, yet awkward. But it had been a while for her, too. She couldn't, though, because if she did meet back up with her partner, it would feel like a betrayal, even though they were separated.

A scratching noise and a gurgle came from across the room. Whirling to the side, Cate spotted a dark shadow. As it crept closer with sloshing movements, it wasn't a shadow at all, but something monstrous with blackened skin peeling off in places. It dragged itself across the floorboards by its forearms, half on its stomach, inching toward them, leaving pools of blood on the wood. Deacon snatched Cate's hand and tugged her toward the stairs. "I think being down here for the night isn't an option any longer. When I told you my room was safe, I meant it, so just trust me."

She tightened her grip on his hand and moved faster, flinging him up the stairs with her. Behind her she could hear suctioning sounds and loud groans reverberating off the walls, growing in number. Cate snatched the tape player from the hallway and stopped in front of Deacon's room. Howls boomed from her room, so she would avoid that for now until it was safe for her to grab a few of her tools. Hurriedly, she followed him into his space, slamming the door behind them and locking it.

"These aren't ghosts," Cate whispered. "I don't know what they are, but this is not what I usually deal with."

"I think they're demons." Deacon sighed and lit a candle. "My own personal hell, I guess."

"You may want to try moving then." In the morning, Cate might need to meet with a priest.

"I'm not moving. This is my home." He tugged open a drawer and grabbed a few incense sticks. He lit them with a lighter, the lavender scent hitting her nostrils. "This will keep them farther away."

"How do you know that?" When she wanted to keep spirits at bay and rest for the night from seeing or hearing them, she always used lavender.

"A friend once told me." Deacon's shoulders slumped as he sank onto the bed and stared out the window, his hands squeezing his knees.

The look in his eyes... She knew right away what kind of friend he meant. The same sort of one she missed. It wasn't just a friend, it was either an ex-girlfriend, or maybe an ex-fiancée, or even an ex-wife. Something with the letter "X" in front of it, unless the woman was dead...

Cate remembered the empty picture frames sprawled on top of the desk, and she focused on them, confirming that this person was much more than a friend who he still missed yet didn't want to see.

Maybe he did need to get over someone, just as she needed to. Maybe she could use a distraction from her heartache. From her *headache*. Maybe...

The thought of leaving Deacon looking like that and returning to her room with nothing but her countless notes and tedious recordings wasn't what she wanted in that moment, even if the spirit had left.

Studying him now, his beautiful features in the candlelight, she wanted to be reckless for once in her life. Cate wanted to think of anything but ghosts and spirits—she wanted to shut out the sounds that the house had been making, wanted to feel alive and whole, instead of discarded and forgotten. It didn't matter that she'd only just met Deacon—she needed to feel his skin against hers.

Taking a deep breath, Cate walked across the room until she stood only inches from Deacon. When his gaze met hers, a thread of a connection started to form there, the beginning of something that could be good for the two of them.

"I've been burned, too." She reached out to lift his chin. Deacon's eyes looked almost haunted, melancholic. "Maybe..." she said. "Just for tonight ... we can both forget."

He nodded once, swallowing hard. Something like relief filled his gaze then, and a ghost of a smile formed. Tonight they could drown in the comfort of the other without shame or regret. People did it all the time, even though this would be a first for her to rebound so quickly.

Deacon's fingers trembled as he brought his hand to her cheek, tentatively, his touch feather-light. And then, as if he'd been waiting to do it since he'd first met her, his lips were on hers.

Cate gasped at the realization of how cold she'd felt all day, how incredibly good Deacon's warmth was, as if by his touch alone she would never feel frigid again. And in that moment, she didn't want anyone else—didn't even *think* of anyone else.

His fingers were unbuttoning her shirt, hers were at his waistband, and piece after piece, their clothing fell to the floor until nothing was left between them but skin. Deacon's eyes never left hers, and she missed the touch of his lips every second they weren't against her own. Gripping her waist, Deacon easily lifted her to lie beneath him, his movements as natural as breathing, as if they'd done this a million times. And he began to kiss her until she thought she would lose her mind from the pleasure of it. He kissed every place on her body as if he knew it as well as his own, teasing her, making her moan and beg with pleasure until his lips found hers once more, his eyes dancing with triumph.

"Keep touching me like you want me to always stay," she panted. "And fuck me as though we don't have enough time."

His lips met hers again. "If you do the same," he murmured.

Cate nodded, reaching for him, impatient, and Deacon's hands continued their exploring along her skin—her breasts, her hips, her legs. Unable to wait another second, she grabbed his buttocks and dug her fingernails in, gasping with pleasure as, finally, he slammed inside her. His lips locked on hers as he moved within her, too gently, too carefully, and Cate wanted more. She hardly recognized herself as she wrapped her legs around Deacon and rolled him onto his back, increasing their pace as he gripped her hips, his head falling back, his eyes closing.

When the pleasure struck her, crashing through her in heavenly waves, Cate's eyes fluttered from the intensity, the relief. Deacon groaned, and the sound filled Cate with renewed euphoria as he rolled her over, as if she were weightless. It was his turn to take charge then.

Her fingers digging into his back while he thrust.

His body quaking as he groaned once more.

Finally spent, they stared at each other, chests heaving, Deacon smiling lazily. Cate blinked in surprise at the sudden realization that she hadn't thought of her old partner once. Not one time had her mind been filled with anything—or anyone—other than Deacon.

"So beautiful," he whispered.

Before she could respond, a loud hiss stirred outside the door. They both jerked up, and she noticed the incense had gone out. Deacon groaned as he tore himself away to light another stick.

Cate curled onto her side, turning away from him. Should she feel ashamed of herself? She didn't. In fact, she wanted to do it all over again. When she felt the mattress dip beside her, she could've stayed where she was, but instead she chose to roll over and press her head against Deacon's chest, gathering more of his warmth. She then closed her eyes and drifted to sleep before she had to remember why she was in this bed, at this mansion—to do her job. But for the night, she'd forget this one time.

When Cate opened her eyes it was still dark, only a sliver of light filtering through the window. In sleep, Deacon's breaths came out heavy, like this was the first time he'd slept in ages. She couldn't go back to sleep, not even if she wanted to.

Pushing the covers away from her body, Cate got up from the bed and put on her clothes before heading to begin her work. This is why she'd come here, not to stay naked in bed with a stranger, even though she already missed his warmth. She picked up the tape player and rewound it, then pressed play. Her day would need to be focused on this, especially since it involved things she'd never dealt with before. There was a first for everything.

As she listened intently, Cate kept the volume low and held it up beside her ear, careful not to disturb Deacon. For a long while, there was nothing, until static flickered. She brought the player as close to her ear as she could, paying close attention as the static formed words.

"Cate, I love you." Her eyes opened wide and she yanked the recorder away from her ear. Not because they were words of a ghost, but because she recognized the voice. Her gaze focused on a still-sleeping Deacon.

It wasn't his words that scared her, but because of the emotion swelling in her chest—she loved him, too. But she couldn't, not after just meeting him, not because they'd shared their bodies with one another. But because...

"Stop it," she whispered to herself.

Cate stared at the pictureless frames and tore open the drawer, finding rows of envelopes with her name written across. Her hand trembled as she sifted farther and noticed a stack of turned over photographs at the bottom. She picked the pictures up and flipped them over.

Her lips parted when her eyes met Deacon, because they were not only of him, but of him and another woman. One she knew very well. Blonde pixie-cut hair, wide-set green eyes, freckles. Her. Cate's heart beat so quickly that she couldn't breathe, not at all.

The photographs were plucked from her hand. Cate hadn't even heard him get up from the bed because she was so lost on what was happening. Deacon placed the pictures back into the drawer and shut it.

His gaze met hers, his body trembling as much as hers was.

"Who is your boyfriend, Cate?" he whispered.

The back of her head pounded as she recalled things. She didn't have an ex-boyfriend—it was only ever Deacon, but he'd been separated from her, because he hadn't come that day. "You are," she murmured. The whole time had been a blur—she'd told herself that she didn't want to think about his name, but the fact was that she *couldn't* remember it, or his face, clearly. Until now.

"Do you remember?" His face was filled with so much hope that Cate could barely breathe as her heart pounded and pounded even more.

"Everything."

His lips pressed against hers and he wrapped his arms around her while she did the same to his waist, only she hugged him harder.

She was the first to pull away, her eyes meeting his again. "I'm-I'm not alive. I was murdered."

He nodded. "That's why you're here, still with unfinished business."

She'd been hired for a ghost hunt—the woman in her mid-fifties had claimed that spirits had been haunting her home, leaving claw marks on her skin. When Cate had found a dead body in one of the closets that had been stabbed and clawed, she'd tried to call the police. Cate knew the client had done this, but before the police had picked up, the woman had smacked Cate in the back of the head with a bat, killing her. Deacon was supposed to have gone, too, but he'd had to work that day at his other job. He'd told her to postpone it until the next day when he could come. They always went as a team. But she hadn't listened—she'd itched too much to hurry and help the woman solve her problem. In the end, she should've waited for him.

"And you, you're still alive." She brought her hand to his cheek, feeling the softness, the warmth.

Deacon shook his head. "No."

"No?"

"After you died, I found your ghost, but you had forgotten me and wouldn't leave that house to pass on to the other side. You were so alone, and I, I was so alone, too."

"So you..."

Tears spilled from his eyes and down his cheeks. "I let myself fall from the cliff outside. The things in this house are here now because of me killing myself. They want to torment me, not you. And they aren't ghosts, but something much darker, and I can't get rid of them."

Our house. This was our house together. The mansion was how she'd met him, when he'd inherited it at only eighteen after his parents died. She'd helped him rid the house of their spirits. Soon after, they became friends, partners, lovers, and then they were to be married.

"How do you remember?" Cate asked.

"I always remember," he murmured, running his hand softly up and down her back. "I've lured you here time and time again with each letter. Then I prepare you the meals in hopes that you will question why nothing has a taste."

"I don't know. I think it's because I felt you just didn't know how to cook. But when we kissed, I could taste you, and if I couldn't have done that, I would've certainly stopped to question what was going on." She couldn't recall any other time she'd been here after her death. There were only the memories of her past life with him and waking the morning before. "And you have to do this every time to get me to remember?"

"Most of the time, you never remember. Most of the time, you think I'm a murderer or something else."

She brought her hands to her mouth and laughed. "That was you moving the planchette on the Ouija, wasn't it?"

He chuckled then, too, taking a step back from her. "It's because I'm so desperate! There isn't enough time for me to woo you with lullabies, so I have to think up ways, like with the Ouija. There have been times where I've even tried to take you from the other house and run away with you, but the places where we died always call us back the next morning."

Her brow furrowed and she took a step forward. "What do you mean?"

"The sun's coming. You'll forget me soon and will return to where you were murdered."

"While you still remember everything." It wasn't a question, because she knew.

Deacon nodded. "I want you to move on to the other side and be happy."

"I think I know what my unfinished business is."

"What is that?"

"To stay here with you for all eternity." She ran her finger over his bottom lip.

"Oh, sweet Cate, I love you so much." Deacon reached for both her hands and interlaced their fingers. "But don't stay for me."

"Why? So I can truly be miserable?" She grabbed his face and pressed her lips to his, kissing him hard, desperate, with tears sliding down her face, just as the sun started to rise. "Make me remember. Show me the pictures first next time."

"I've done that, and you go off running every time."

Cate could feel herself being torn away from him. She wrapped her arms around his waist, gripping him so tight that she wouldn't be forced away.

But she was.

Deacon stood shaking, feeling only air as his hands wrapped around to his back, holding himself tight. He dropped to his knees and pressed his hands to his eyes and let himself cry, but he couldn't afford to do it for too long. The night before had been one of his best memories since they'd been alive together, and now Cate was gone. The previous night, he remembered her body against his, her hands clasping his, and he would do this again and again for her to come back to him, because that was what she wished.

He loved her so damn much. He'd find a better way to do things, and somehow, he swore to himself, he'd get them both in a better place.

Quietly, he sat at the desk and pulled from the drawer one of the envelopes with her name written across. Deacon lifted a blank sheet of paper and took a pen in his other hand before scrawling the same note he did every time, beginning with her name. *Cate.*

This time, he hoped she would be able to stay to help him fight.

Dearest Dorin,

I hope you enjoyed my tale. The thing about happy endings is ... sometimes we have to wait. In the end of my capture with Bogdi, I may have saved myself, but you were there when I stumbled out. Even if you weren't physically in the darkness with me, you were there inside my heart. Your beautiful demon spirit was with me then as it will always be. As for Cate and Deacon, we may not know the end of their story now, same as our own, but one day I believe they will survive, just as we have thus far.

Love Always,
Clementine

Thank you so much for reading Dearest Clementine: Dark and Romantic Monstrous Tales and Dearest Dorin: A Romantic Ghostly Tale!

Subscribe to Candace's Awesome Newsletter for exclusive content!

Also From Candace Robinson

Wicked Souls Duology
Vault of Glass
Bride of Glass

Marked by Magic Duology
The Bone Valley
Merciless Stars

Cruel Curses Trilogy
Clouded By Envy
Veiled By Desire
Shadowed By Despair

Faeries of Oz Series
Lion (Short Story Prequel)
Tin
Crow

Ozma
Tik-Tok

Cursed Hearts Duology
Lyrics & Curses
Music & Mirrors

Letters Duology
Dearest Clementine: Dark and Romantic Monstrous Tales
Dearest Dorin: A Romantic Ghostly Tale

Campfire Fantasy Tales Series
Lullaby of Flames
A Layer Hidden
The Celebration Game
Mirror, Mirror

These Vicious Thorns: Tales of the Lovely Grim
Between the Quiet
Hearts Are Like Balloons
Bacon Pie
Avocado Bliss

Vampires in Wonderland
Rav (Short Story Prequel)
Maddie
Chess
Knave

Once Upon A Wicked Villain Series
Spindle of Sin

Acknowledgments

I've always wanted to do a collection of stories that involved aspects of horror entangled with romance. They are just two of my favorite things ever!

As always, I'd love to thank all the readers who read this book. Hopefully you guys found as much enjoyment reading it as I did writing it!

I'd also like to thank Alexa Whitewolf with her awesome editing skills and K.M. Robinson for putting a beautiful cover together that matches these stories perfectly!

Donna Weiss, Gerardo Delgadillo, Amber R. Duell, Amber Hodges, Victoria Robinson, Patricia Thibodeaux, Kattie Sivley, Erica Burden, S.G.D. Singh and Elle Beaumont. Thank you guys so much for taking the time to read my story early and helping to make it better!

What would a world be like without those we love? So Nate and Arwen, always remember that you two share my heart! Mom, you're always there when I need you, and I love you!

To everyone else who thinks horror romance should be a thing, then I crown you with multiple cool points for believing that monsters can love too!

About the Author

Candace Robinson spends her days consumed by words and hoping to one day find her own DeLorean time machine. Her life consists of avoiding migraines, admiring Bonsai trees, watching classic movies, and living with her husband and daughter in Texas—where it can be forty degrees one day and eighty the next.

Connect with Candace:

Website:
https://authorcandacerobinson.wordpress.com/
Facebook: https://www.facebook.com/literarydust
Twitter: https://twitter.com/literarydust
Instagram:
https://www.instagram.com/candacerobinsonbooks/
Goodreads:
https://www.goodreads.com/author/show/16541001.Candace_Robinson or ignore that and just try searching for Candace Robinson!

Printed in Poland
by Amazon Fulfillment
Poland Sp. z o.o., Wrocław

36252267R00127